Between Danger and Desire

An Enemies to Lovers, Thrilling Dark Romance

Nicole Shaw

Copyright © 2023 by Nicole Shaw

All rights reserved.

No portion of this book may be reproduced in any form without written permission from the publisher or author, except as permitted by U.S. copyright law.

Have you ever experienced the mysterious magnetism of people forbidden to you, those you shouldn't want but do? An erratic desire thrives in you, flirts with your heart, and tortures your thoughts.

Hired as an assistant at my brother's company, I wasn't prepared for my new boss, Sebastian, my brother's best friend.

Fresh out of the Navy, he was hard-headed, damaged, and...

I wanted to hate him. But his dazzling looks muddled my mind and displaced my sanity.

He'd pull me in, push me away, then reel me back, twisting my emotions until I was too dizzy to see anything but him.

So I embraced his torment.

And just as we began fanning lust's embers, a threat from his past resurfaced. Running away wasn't an option. Or maybe the terror enhancing the passion kept me from leaving. Either way, I was caught between danger and desire.

I love to jump into a story completely blind and let the words surprise me. But I understand that not everyone else does. This book does contain some things that could be upsetting to people. If you feel you are one of those people please keep reading for a trigger warning list. If you want to dive into it, go right to chapter 1 now.

Between Danger and Desire is a very emotional and exciting story. It is strictly fiction and I do not condone or promote any of the actions or behaviors in this book. Main triggers will be PTSD, Danger, Dom/Sub role play, some Violence. For a more detailed list see the next page.

Sebastian:
He is a former soldier with PTSD: a very brief mention of self harm, and descriptive memories of a fire.
Talk of an illegal sex trafficking ring.
Possessive

Laura:
Erotic asphyxiation (breath play)
Anal
Safe Word
Bondage
Punishment/spanking
Kidnapping
Non-consensual touch (very brief)

Contents

1. Laura — 1
2. Sebastian — 5
3. Laura — 9
4. Laura — 13
5. Laura — 17
6. Sebastian — 22
7. Sebastian — 26
8. Laura — 30
9. Laura — 44
10. Sebastian — 48
11. Laura — 53
12. Laura — 58
13. Sebastian — 62
14. Sebastian — 67

15.	Laura	71
16.	Sebastian	76
17.	Laura	79
18.	Laura	87
19.	Laura	93
20.	Sebastian	98
21.	Laura	104
22.	Sebastian	108
23.	Laura	112
24.	Sebastian	115
25.	Laura	118
26.	Laura	122
27.	Laura	128
28.	Laura	133
Epilogue		138

1
Laura

I wanted everybody walking the pavement thirty-two stories below to know Sebastian Delarossi had his fat cock inside me. If I'd only known he was going to push me against the floor-to-ceiling window, flip me around, and thrust tingles from my pussy to next week's dreams, I would've handed out binoculars to all of Austin, sent emails, and posted flyers at every corner from here to Topeka. Then millions of people could gather on the street to see the rapids rushing down my legs while I was fed cock by the pound from a man sexier than any model you could invent.

Nearly breathless but still fogging up the glass muffling my moans, I teetered on my toenails because each thrust sent me closer to the moon. He'd yank me back by the hips and slam his dick into me as quickly as he pulled back, no pause and no restraint, just one momentous pounding, an epic fuck so earth-shattering I thought the airplane buzzing overhead might fall from the sky and crash through the roof. I wished it would. Then I could pull the pilot out of the cockpit and say, "Look! Look who's fucking me."

"Laura—did you hear me?"

"Huh? Oh, sorry. I was just trying to remember if I turned the stove off this morning."

"I don't know about the other places you've worked, but here, we don't daydream. Will that be a problem for you?"

"It won't happen again."

"I hope not. I don't like repeating myself. And this is the last time I'll ever do it. So listen very carefully: I don't want you to be my assistant. I want nothing to do with you. And I'll do everything in my power to ensure you don't last. Yet I won't fire you. Instead, I'll make your time here very difficult. And I won't stop until you quit. If you and Cooper want to play games, so will I."

"Do whatever you want. You won't get rid of me. I'm a very patient woman. Besides, I'll be so good at my job you won't want me to leave."

"We'll see about that. Be here tomorrow at eight o'clock, sharp. On your way out, speak to my secretary. Sharon will fill you in on your responsibilities and give you a copy of my schedule and enough paperwork to keep you busy until Christmas."

"I won't let you down." I stood and extended a hand for a shake. "Fine, be that way." I turned, stuttered a step, then glanced over my shoulder. "See you at home, boss."

"Excuse me? What the hell is that supposed to mean?"

"Cooper didn't tell you? I'll be staying with you two until I get settled into the city and save enough for my own place."

The next morning.

"Mr. Delarossi, I'm incredibly sorry for being late. I didn't hear my alarm. I promise, it won't happen again. In fact, from now on, I'll arrive thirty minutes early. I swear I will. Please, don't fire me."

He looked so powerful sitting at his desk. The intensity in his eyes was daunting but eerily attractive. The man was sculpted to perfection, undoubtedly one of the most beautiful men I'd ever seen.

"I'm not going to fire you, Laura."

"Really, you're not?" Deep breath. "I mean, thank you."

"I told you, I won't fire you. This will end when you quit, which—you will do, mark my words. In the meantime, don't be late again because I won't be so lenient the next time. Understood?"

Something about his domineering tone stirred my nerves and twisted my emotions. My mouth went dry, and swallowing was painful.

"Y-yes, sir. Understood. Do you need anything before I go?"

"A cup of coffee. Black. That means no sugar and no milk. Just pour the coffee and bring it to me. Got it? Or do you need me to write it down in crayon?"

"Coming right up."

I poured the coffee and brought it to him.

He sipped skeptically. I studied his expression, my fingers crossed behind me.

He spat the coffee back into the cup and pushed it away.

"It has a hair in it. And this mug is dirty."

"But I—"

"You know what, forget it. Go back to your closet. Book my meetings and send them over to my email."

"I knew it was a closet. How rude. You mean to tell me that there's not one empty office within these thirty-two floors? I highly doubt that."

"Actually, there are several offices available, all with windows, too. One of them even has a nice view of the homeless encampment in the alley. But you won't step foot in any of them. And the only reason I gave you the supplies closet was because Jarrod refuses to give up his mop closet on account of it having a drain."

"You know what? It's fine, really. The supplies closet is quiet. I like quiet. Yesterday, I even had the pleasure of hearing men groaning in the bathroom I share a wall with. And it was comforting to know I wasn't alone."

"That's the spirit. Now beat it. I've got a call to make or something. Oh, and Laura? . . . Don't fuck up my meetings, or your next office will be in a cardboard box with filthy Fred and his minions in the alleyway."

Walking through the hallway, I kept my head down, but people couldn't take a hint.

"So you're the new assistant. I'm Bianca Hart. And this is Jake Sanders." They each motioned for a handshake. Bianca's fingernails were long and pink.

Jake had dirt under his thumbnail. "I work in IT. Bianca's in HR."

"I'm Laura Anderson. It's nice to meet you guys."

Bianca: "Wait, as in Cooper Anderson? Your brother owns this company, and you chose to work as an assistant?"

"It's a long story." Kill me now.

"Well, you have it coming for you—I'll tell you that," Bianca said. "Word on the street is he fired his last assistant just because she came back a minute late from her lunch break."

"I heard she put sugar in his coffee," said Jake. "The man has severe anger issues."

"I'm sure he's not that bad," I said.

"Your face says otherwise."

"It was just a minor disagreement—no biggie."

"All I can say is good luck. But don't worry. We'll help you survive his torturous ways."

"Really, you'd help me?" Big smile—really sell it.

"Of course. I like you, and unlike the other snobbish assistants, I actually want you to stay." She doesn't even know me.

"Yeah, me too."

"Thank you. You're both so kind."

2
Sebastian

It usually starts with me in a steel box similar to a shipping container, only a third of the size, and there are no shipping containers on Navy ships.

It's not supposed to make sense.

There's a spotlight in the container's middle, but I can't trace its source. Smoke rises from a concrete floor and thickens quickly. As the smoke pervades the container, I shrink into a corner. I know what's coming. I've been here before.

I pull the neck of my shirt over my mouth and nose, coughing. I can see nothing but the smoke, and as it blackens, the image flickers with a screech: white noise. I'm crouched on my old bottom bunk, still holding my shirt over my face, a centerfold above me. The screams that live inside my head wake the dead. I can't move. Another flicker happens. The sound of nails on a chalkboard. The top bunk is ablaze. A wall of fire creeps toward me. There is no way out.

Murray and Dobbs stumble through the flames. They're not on fire. Ashes and sparks trail them as they walk. Murray's face slides off. Dobbs's arms are burnt and bubbling. I can see the bones from his hands to his elbows, and pieces crumble and fall. He reaches to touch me and says raspily. "Help me." Then the room is engulfed.

I wake up in the container. Its walls are blanketed with flames. From the darkness that shouldn't exist, several of my old shipmates walk toward me. I'm hot and coughing, gasping. They're crispy from head to toe. Their sailor uniforms are still visible in spots, just patches of blackened white melted to their bones and charred skin. I don't know who's who. Their scalps are missing, and brain matter oozes from their heads. They surround me. One of them carries a red can of gasoline. Nobody speaks, just heavy breathing, like a collective death rattle.

They form a semicircle around me and creep closer, their eyes bloodshot and nearly falling out of their heads. One of them pours gasoline on me. It's Murray. I know because he has a gold tooth. And it's always Murray, yet I always seem surprised by the revelation. He flips open the Zippo I gifted him at his wedding. He sparks a flame and holds the lighter above me, looking at me as if I'm already dead. He calls me a coward, then lets go of the Zippo. I freefall through an orange sky and smell brimstone.

I jolted awake, screaming. I held my chest and coughed to clear the unreal smoke from my lungs. It could've been worse, much worse. In an alternate version, Murray would slit my throat and jam the gas can's nozzle into the bloody opening.

I sat on the bed's edge, comparing the burning ship I'd survived to the imaginary one carrying the dead. I reached between the mattresses, pulled out the box cutter, and slid down my briefs. On my right leg's inner thigh, I carved a two-inch line between the others: some scars, some scabbed over. Blood ran down my leg, and a droplet hit the carpet. My dick was hard. I grabbed a bandage from the drawer in the nightstand, covered the wound, and went downstairs.

The real fire had been a retaliation to me procuring a thumb drive with enough information to dismantle a global crime syndicate specializing in trafficking women and turning them into sex slaves. The traffickers had threatened to kill me if I didn't return the drive. I refused because—fuck them.

SEBASTIAN

My screams had once traveled down the hall and woken Cooper. So I'd recounted a nightmare to give him an understanding of what I was dealing with but avoided the gory details. He'd suggested I see a psychiatrist, which I thought was absurd. I didn't need a shrink, and I sure as fuck didn't need his sister looking after me. What did he think—that I might off myself? So what if I did?

I switched on the fluorescent lights in the gym, ignored my face in the mirrored walls, and went straight to the canvas punching bag in the far corner. I beat on it until the sun shone through the skylight.

Drenched in sweat, my shirt stuck to my body. I pulled it off, draped it over a barbell, and headed to the kitchen for water.

Laura chomped into an apple and adorably froze mid-bite, her teeth buried in its red skin. She gazed at my shirtless, sweaty chest and blushed. I watched her with the same intensity she did me, clenching my jaw at the skimpy night dress hugging her body.

She unearthed her teeth without taking her intended bite. "Good morning. I thought I was the only one awake."

"Clearly not." I went to the fridge and grabbed a bottled water.

She was still staring when I turned and lowered my head, swallowing my last gulp of water. Her eyes were captivating and alluring, but I saw them for what they were, a warning label. I knew that look. I often had to stop myself from making a similar face whenever near her.

"Cancel my appointments for the next few days. I'll be out of town and unreachable."

"Is everything okay?"

"It's nothing. Just business."

"Is there any way I can help?"

"Yeah, you can go to the office and cancel my appointments like I asked you to. For suck's sake, know your damn place."

"Okay. I was only asking."

"Well don't. Just do as you're told."

"I'll contact you if I need anything."

"Don't bother. If you have any questions, my secretary will answer them."

"Yes, boss. Are you leaving right now?"

"Yes."

"You're not going to eat something first?"

"What are you, my nanny?"

3
Laura

I hadn't heard anything from Sebastian since he'd left the house a few days ago. Cooper told me not to worry because Sebastian leaving without sharing his whereabouts wasn't uncommon. I could easily call him on the phone, but he said not to. I didn't want to bother him. Yet I couldn't stop wondering why he abruptly left the house.

I knew nothing about him. He was so secretive and revealed nothing of his personal life. All I knew was he served in the Navy for twenty years and was discharged a year ago for reasons unknown to anybody except maybe my brother. But he was unlikely to disclose personal information regarding his best friend.

When I wasn't worrying about Sebastian, I daydreamed, remembering my interview with him and how his cold demeanor complemented his domineering attitude. Sexy and powerful, he demanded respect wherever he went and could have anything he wanted whenever he wanted it. I loved men like that. I found it incredibly hot. Unfortunately, in his eyes, I was his best friend's little sister and nothing more. Not to mention, he was 17 years older than me. He probably wouldn't even notice me if I wasn't his assistant.

According to the rumors, he gave attention only to women of mass sophistication, models blessed with the body type every man desires. These women practically worshipped him. And they knew the rules: no dating or relationships. His encounters with women were strictly sexual.

"Laura—I have an idea." I couldn't see Jake because my back faced the door, but I knew that soft voice.

"Hold on. I'm almost done with this email."

He sat on my desk's edge and took in the room, a pen tucked behind one ear. His shirt sleeves were rolled up to his elbows.

"Annd . . . done. What's this great idea of yours?"

"There's a great great pizza place over on 6th Street. Maybe you and I could sneak off and grab a bite. Then we could stop at the Musuem of the Weird after and check out all the creepy wax statues."

"I shouldn't. I have so much work to do. Sebastian keeps piling it on. I swear he invents random things for me to do." I wanted to go with Jake. No, I didn't. But I did. You understand. "Anyway, it's not our lunch break."

"Oh, come on. Your brother owns this company. You can do whatever you want. And your boss isn't even here. I don't see the problem."

"I don't know."

"It's gonna be fun, trust me. Besides, you must need the air. It's so stuffy in here. Maybe over lunch you can explain why Sebastian put your office in a closet?"

"We can talk about anything except Sebastian."

"So you'll go?"

"It is tempting." I briefly studied the ceiling. "Okay, I'll go. But not a word of this to anyone. Okay?"

He pursed his lips. "Not a word." Then he pretended to throw away a key.

"Why are you staring at me like that?"

"No reason. You're just so beautiful."

I muttered a thank you while grabbing my purse from the concrete floor. I wasn't good at receiving compliments, much less from an attractive man.

"Going somewhere?" said a husky voice behind us. Then Sebastian's face appeared. I felt stupid. Guilty. Smitten. Embarrassed. So many emotions collided inside me and disordered my thoughts.

"N-no sir. There are a few, uh, documents I needed to collect from her. But she doesn't have them. So I'll be on my way." Jake scurried off.

Sebastian waited for me to speak, letting the silence linger. His stubbled chin and weary eyes almost made him look more sad than stressed.

"Welcome back, Mr. Delarossi. I had no idea you were coming home today."

"Is this what you've been up to, flirting with your coworkers instead of working? Do I pay you to flirt?"

"Flirt?"

"Don't play dumb with me. It's unbecoming." He was so still and solid. He didn't even blink. "I overheard you and Sanders making plans to leave. And you blushed when he called you beautiful. That's called flirting where I'm from."

"It wasn't like that at all."

"Oh no? I suppose he didn't just pull out your chair and hold your coat, either."

It was difficult to control myself. I wanted so badly to touch him, to feel his embrace, to wake up next to him and brush my bare legs against his, then pinch myself.

"You wanna know the truth?" I stepped toward him. "I have been working—a lot. And guess what? I've had to stop myself from calling you multiple times because I've been worried sick about you. Not that you care."

He moved closer to me. I could smell his sweat and moved back, taking baby steps until my butt touched my desk.

"If you're trying to make me forget I caught you getting cute with Sanders, you failed miserably."

My shoulders sank. I felt like a dog must when being scolded for messing on the carpet. So much shame. Yet the desire I harbored for him raged, which only emphasized the shame. How could one man elicit such an array of emotions?

"Don't let this happen again. Understood?"

I tucked in my chin. "Understood."

4
Laura

Jake had apologized for running off. It wasn't an issue, anyway, though I accepted his apology as if it were. Then we made plans for the evening. An ice cream date seemed childish, yet I was looking forward to it.

I wore a blue, long sleeve mini dress with an open back. I was skeptical about wearing it because I didn't want to give Jake the wrong impression. But the dress was so cute that I couldn't stop myself from wearing it. I admired myself in the mirror and winked.

Downstairs, Cooper and Sebastian were engrossed in a football game and yelling at the TV. Did they think the players could hear them? I've never understood that. And I didn't understand how Sebastian made everything look so friggin sexy. It was effortless for him. If anyone had asked me last month what the sluttiest thing a man could wear was, I would've said sweatpants. Not now, though, because Sebastian wore sweats daily and flustered me.

Sensing my presence, they snapped their heads back and took a good look.

Cooper said, "Well, don't you look amazing. Hot date?"

Sebastian's face appeared surprised while his eyes, despite studying me, seemed to feign indifference. I smirked brattily, taunting him.

"Yes, Coop. I'm going on a date."

Sebastian turned back to the TV, though the way his head was cocked told me he wasn't listening to the game.

"Who's the lucky guy?" said Cooper.

"Just someone from work."

Sebastian's head spun around. "Tell me it's not Sanders."

"It is. So what?"

"You know him?"

"He works in IT. You should know this. He's harmless but an absolute bore."

"How would you know? You don't talk to anybody. You've probably never even had a conversation with Jake. And for the record, he's very interesting."

Sebastian snickered.

"Alright, have fun," Cooper said. "Be safe."

"Be safe. Got it." I waved halfheartedly while walking past the backs of their heads. "Bye."

When I arrived at the ice cream shop, Jake was patiently waiting, leaning against his Subaru, his arms and legs crossed. I apologized for being late. We ordered: cookies and cream for Jake and coconut for me. We strolled around a nearby park and told polished versions of our lives. He tried to hold my hand. I tried not to think about Sebastian. Time leaped forward. He said he'd never before asked a girl out. I said my feet hurt. It was one a.m. I let him kiss me under the flickering light of the empty lot at the ice cream shop. Just a peck. Then we parted ways with a wave from our cars and had our thoughts.

I woke up hungry and remembered I hadn't eaten dinner last night. Jake had wanted to stop at an all-night diner, but I was too tired, I'd said.

Downstairs, I was licking whipped cream off my fingertip while cooking a pancake, wondering whether one was enough, when an intruder walked in. Not that kind.

"Hey, there. You must be Laura." She opened the fridge. Already, I didn't like her. Her manner was too casual. You would've thought she lived here.

Worse, she was without pants and wearing one of Sebastian's Under Armour t-shirts.

"I'm sorry, you are?"

"Viviane. I'm a friend of Sebas."

"Sebas?"

She placed a bottled water on the counter, pulled an elastic off her wrist, and tied back her hair. "Sebastian, silly. Who else would I be talking about?" Even her laugh was annoying. I couldn't think of a response and didn't have to because Sebastian walked in, all swagger, shirtless. I wanted to crawl into his sweatpants and change my mailing address.

"Sebas!" She wrapped her arms around his neck and kissed him for show. "I was just getting some water when I ran int—"

"Why're you still here? I thought I asked you to leave?"

She pouted. "Excuse me? Who do you think you are talking to like that? Do you think you can just fuck me and throw me away?"

Okay, I definitely didn't need to know that. Awkward. And thinking about them having sex while I was out last night hurt my head. But why?

"Leave, Viviane. I'll call you later."

"Unbelievable." She stormed away, intentionally bumping her shoulder against Sebastian's arm. "Prick."

The front door slammed shut. I wondered if she knew she wasn't wearing pants.

"She didn't deserve to be treated like that. You could've been nicer."

"In case you haven't noticed, I'm not a nice person. I don't do sweet and emotional. I won't hold your hand or buy you flowers and chocolate. I don't cuddle and spoon. And I'm definitely not the type of man you bring home to your parents. I fuck, and I fuck hard. I fuck because it makes me feel powerful, in control, and the rush of the fuck is better than anything love can offer. But I fuck with a purpose. I fuck till it hurts. I fuck to forget. I fuck for the fuck of it. I fuck, Laura, that's it. Then I leave. That's who I am."

I'd paused my fork an inch from my mouth. The triangled bite of pancake I'd neatly cut had dropped to the tiled floor. He stood so close I could feel his body's warmth radiating from his bare chest. He leaned his head in, almost as if he were about to kiss me. "Now you know the kind of man I am."

My chest heaved. My head was light. I had to take a step back. Then he moved forward, pushing me back until my butt bumped into the counter. Deja vu happened. Except in this version, he wouldn't take his eyes off me. He seemed fully aware of the effect he had on me. He enjoyed it.

His index finger touched my bottom lip, so gently. I didn't know he had it in him. Anticipating what he might do next fluttered my heart. My breaths shortened. He swiped the finger across my lip. I would undoubtedly fantasize about this later, for days, weeks, months, probably forever. Then he pulled the finger away. And—hole-ee-shit. How dumb was I? It was just . . . I had whipped cream on my lip. And he'd brushed it off.

I was dizzy from desire and spinning emotions. Was he being nice or just toying with me? I remained mute, afraid to exist, fearful of what I might say. I couldn't process anything. My brain refused to cooperate with me.

He sucked the whipped cream off his finger while watching my eyes try not to close. Then he pulled away and transformed into his usual self. He grabbed an apple from the fruit basket near the stove. "There's a business party Monday night. It's nothing serious, just a small party hosted by one of our investors. Just giving you a heads-up, so you can prepare for it. Your attendance is mandatory. No questions asked. Got it?" He bit into the apple. "Good. I'll see you later."

A cold shower, that was what I needed.

5
Laura

"I don't know—it feels like my boobs are about to pop out of this dress any second." I palmed my breasts, gave them a lift and a drop.

"Try the other one, the black one," Bianca said.

I went back into the changing room and closed the door.

"So, you and Jake, huh."

"We're just friends."

"That's not what he thinks. I couldn't get him to shut up. He was all Laura this, and Laura that. You should have seen his face."

"It was nothing. We hung out, ate ice cream, and talked. That's all."

"It was clearly more than that to him."

"Well, there was a kiss. It was brief and clumsy. I mean—he's really sweet, but...."

"He's too sweet."

"Basically, yeah. And he reminds me of every guy I've ever dated. Just blah. He would probably run to the pharmacy for me at three a.m. to buy tampons, which is awesome and cute and all. But he also seems the type to call an exterminator to remove a spider from the house. You know what I mean? I'm tired of that. And when we were ordering ice cream the other night, he was so indecisive. For once, I'd like a man who knows what he wants, isn't afraid to climb a ladder to change a light bulb, and likes to take control."

"If I didn't know any better, I'd think you were talking about Sebastian."

"What? No. That's insane. He's an asshole. And my boss."

"Mmhm."

"How do I look?"

"That's the one."

I wore a gold bodycon dress. It shimmered, had spaghetti straps, and a plunging neckline, flaunting the right amount of cleavage. The nude strap-heels I borrowed from Bianca elevated my height by two inches, at least, and made my legs appear longer. Sexier, I hoped. My makeup was perfect, complete with smoky eyes and nude-colored lips.

Just as I finished getting ready, Sebastian texted me. He was downstairs waiting. I was nervous and excited. I'd put a lot of work into preparing tonight's look and intended to make his head turn. That was the plan, anyway.

Ever since our heated exchange in the kitchen, he seemed only to leave his room when I was in mine. Of course, I saw him at work, where he was crueler than usual. I couldn't determine whether it was part of his scheme to make me quit or if he was distressed. Probably both.

"Evening, boss." I descended the stairs, one deliberate step at a time, keeping my posture straight, my back arched a touch, playing confident.

"Aren't we running late? Or do you need more time to stare at me?" When I walked past him, he muttered, "God, help me," under his breath. Okay, maybe I imagined those words, but whatever he said was in a tone matching that phrase.

His black suit defined his rugged physique. He looked so powerful, strong enough to throw me to the moon. Even his bowtie had a woozy effect on me. It was straight and crisp, yet after staring at it for a minute, waiting for him to remember where he was, I adjusted it for fun. "There. Now you're ready. Shall we?" Who was I?

LAURA

Neither of us spoke on the ride to the party. It was unsettling, to say the least. Except for when I caught him nonchalantly trying to glance at my legs whenever he took a right turn. Having him notice me, as I craved, was flattering but made me anxious.

We drove up a long driveway ending in a cul-de-sac wrapped around a three-tiered fountain. A valet dressed in a red sportcoat with a gold emblem embroidered on its left lapel opened my door. I turned to step out of the car and was stopped. Sebastian had touched my shoulder. The feelings tearing me apart were fear and devastating lust. He told me to stay by his side all night. No problem. He would introduce me to his investors and friends. I could live with that.

The party was a ploy to comfort his investors and gain favor. However, he'd failed to mention the investors were Mr. and Mrs. Levington, Viviane's parents.

My heart stuttered watching the calculated way Viviane flirted with him, touching him every so often as they spoke to her parents. She would place a palm on his chest and laugh, brush off his shoulders, or unnecessarily straighten his bowtie, which infuriated me. I wanted to leave. I was a stranger, out of my element, forgotten, left behind to mingle with the bartender and spectate.

I couldn't take it. So I walked away, weaving through conversations and escaping the crowd. I found a gazebo amid an elaborate garden, took a seat, and listened to the distant murmurs of those who belonged.

He and Viviane were a perfect match. I couldn't believe I'd been so naive, thinking someone like him would settle with the likes of me. He was out of my league, beyond my grasp, yet here I was, nearly crying, pondering the shelf-life of shame. I couldn't live under the same roof as him anymore. No way. It was too much. But where would I go? And how long had I been weeping beneath those twinkling white lights draped from the gazebo?

"Where the hell have you been? I've been looking all over for you. I called five times. For crying out loud, I thought I told you not to leave my side."

"Stop overreacting. You always overreact. I just needed some quiet. Besides, this isn't the office, so quit bossing me around."

"You're my assistant. So you're always on the clock, and I am always the boss of you. If you don't like it—quit. Just fucking quit. It's not that hard. Two words. I. Quit. End of story, move on, go... wait—why are you crying?" He thumbed a tear off my cheek. "What happened to you?" His sympathy felt like charity.

"Nothing. Can we leave? Or are you still busy making small talk with your in-laws?"

"My in-laws?" His forehead wrinkled, part of his act, I presumed. "Is this about Viviane and her parents? The Levingtons are important investors. I must keep a good relationship with them."

"Is that why you're messing around with their daughter?"

"You're ridiculous. I don't have to explain myself to you. Grow the fuck up." He stood, straightened his suit coat, puffed his chest, and raised his shoulders. "You're such a child."

"That's rich coming from you. I'm not the one who avoids people and refuses to own up to their actions. Maybe I am a child, but at least I'm not a coward."

"What the hell are you talking about?"

"Oh, don't play dumb. It doesn't suit you."

"Is this about the other day in the kitchen? What did you think, that I would start making advances at you? That I'd start chasing you? Is that why you dressed so provocatively tonight? Jesus, Laura. You're my best friend's sister. Not to mention, I'm way older than you. And I have zero interest in puppy-love drama."

His relentless contempt for me was unbearable. No, I couldn't stop myself from crying, as hard as I tried. Not helping my emotional state were the lights strung from the gazebo reminding me of Christmas, of happiness and cheer. How sad. Even sadder was my dress reflected the lights in so many shimmers and made me feel prettier than ever. I sobbed with a sniffle that begged for pity. My woe was pathetic.

"Aww, did I hurt your feelings? Have I offended your delicate sensibilities? Well—too bad. Because this is who I am. I warned you, didn't I? Whatever story you've cooked up in that little head of yours is a fantasy. I'm not the guy who'll rescue you from a tower. I can't save you. Get over it. And for fuck's sake, Laura, do us all a favor, and quit. I'll never be any nicer, and you'll never be anybody but you."

"Fuck you." I stormed off, trying hard to shake the earth with each stomp. Instead, it seemed to spin on its axis faster. I was such an idiot, imagining he and I could or would make one another happy and have intimacy. What a joke. I romanticized an asshole and got treated like shit.

6

Sebastian

Tears crowded her face and blurred her makeup. Her knees shook. Her words seemed to bunch up in her throat and flee in nervous gasps. Then she ran off sobbing, and left in her wake a lavender scent I could not shake. Unable to abandon my feelings and rid my eyes of her face, I snagged a bottle of Johnny Blue when the bartender turned his back. Then I returned to the gazebo and drank, alone, trying to reshape my emotions and conform my thoughts into logical reasons not to . . . not to what? What was it I didn't want to do?

Would you believe me if I told you I felt guilty? Because I did. I was an asshole. But what choice did I have? Nothing could ever happen between us. And the best way to ensure we never surpassed the occasional hello was to make her despise me. Still, I felt horrible.

From that night forward, wherever I went and looked, she was there, even when she wasn't. At work and home, she was unavoidable. We'd put our heads down and occasionally wave lazily and mutter a hey. That was it. But she was constantly on my mind. I would catch a whiff of lavender while ordering a coffee and look over my shoulder, only to lose a smile and wish I was somewhere else.

SEBASTIAN

What happened in the kitchen was impulsive, proof of how vulnerable she made me. Now with each interaction we had, my restraint withered more.

Her voice prickled my ears.

"Please, Coop. I don't want to go alone."

"Ask Sebastian to go with you. Look, here he comes now."

I raised a brow, confused. I attempted to wipe the sleep from my eyes, unsure I had heard him correctly.

"Laura wants someone to go grocery shopping with her. I can't. I've got a thing."

I turned on my heels to leave the kitchen.

"Liar. You're just lazy."

"Be that as it may—hey, Sebastian. Come on, man. If you don't go with her, I'll never hear the end of it."

I spun back around, keeping my head low. "Fine." What the fuck? No, no, this was such a bad idea. Had I gone mad? Yes, the answer was yes.

"Yay! We're going to have so much fun. I just have to change real quick. Okay? And you should definitely do the same. Or don't. Sweatpants in public is totally fine."

"She's really something," said Cooper. "You should splash some water on your face. You look like hell. And your breath reeks. Why've you been drinking so much lately?"

"Don't worry about it. I'm fine."

"If you say so."

I wondered whether Laura and I would revisit our night at the party. Maybe for her time had worked its magic. I could never forget it. And I certainly wouldn't mention it.

She was so busy keeping uncomfortable silence at a distance, talking with her hands, that she paid little attention to the road. It was adorable how sometimes she would rub her nose with her palm as a child would. Why? Because there wasn't a movement she made, or a breath she took that didn't excite me. Even the way she sat slightly hunched before the steering wheel with her chin raised to better see over the dashboard moved me. She would nod in response to her own questions, shaking her hoop earrings and drawing my attention to the peach fuzz on her earlobes. I would nod back in awe, struck dumb and defenseless, afraid to breathe.

"What do you think you're doing? That's the worst Pringle's flavor there is." She bunched her face, wrinkling her nose.

"You're crazy. It's the only decent flavor they make."

"No, the original is the best. They taste like McDonald's french fries. Those taste like a French onion dip left out too long at a party. You know—when it gets all crusty and brown around the edges. Eww." She swapped Pringle's cans. Her earrings jiggled with the no she wouldn't let go of. Choose your battles. That's what my mother used to say to me whenever I'd receive detention for fighting.

"Here, let me." I couldn't watch her struggle to push the cart any longer. It was getting heavy and had one uncooperative wheel that wouldn't spin right, so it would take her one or three shoves to get it moving.

"Trust me, the original flavor is the best," she said, continuing a conversation that had died five aisles back. "My parents used to buy it for Cooper and I."

"How are they, anyway? It's been a while since I've seen them."

"They're fine, really enjoying their trip to Australia." She paused. "And what about you?"

"What about me?"

"Your family. How're they?"

"I haven't seen my parents since I went into the Navy."

"That long ago? You must miss them."

"Life happens."

"Why haven't you tried to reach out to them?" She stopped walking. Her face said she was disappointed in me.

"Maybe I'm too embarrassed. The way I left the navy and all." I didn't know why I was telling her this.

"What happened? Tell me. . . . C'mon, Sebastian, talking helps a lot."

"Drop it, Laura. You're not my fucking therapist?"

"Woah, I wasn't trying to be. I was only asking a question."

"What have I told you about asking questions?"

"I'm tired of this. One minute you're nice to me, and the next, you're being a complete asshole. I understand this is part of your plan to make me quit, but—newsflash—it won't happen. And the sooner you accept that, the better. Now, let's go check out. We're done here."

7
Sebastian

The situation concerning the sex traffickers had been a heavy burden for too long. Even when my mind was absorbed with Laura, beneath it all, the trafficking case lurked, twisting my nerves. And if those two things weren't enough to keep me up at night, my nightmares prevented me from getting proper sleep.

"You look like shit," said Cooper, taking a seat beside me on the couch. I snatched the glass of whisky from his hand and downed it.

"I fucking feel like shit." I shook the glass. Ice clinked. I took the last sip, set the glass on the coffee table, and, as I leaned back, I noticed blood seeping through my pants. I squeezed my legs together and placed my hands on my lap.

"Is this about the case? Any new developments?"

"Yeah. Matt just texted me. He's got something. Finally. He's been trying to crack their database for how long now—three months? Damn. It feels like three years. Whatever he's got, it must be big because he'll only tell me in person. I have to be in Colombia the day after tomorrow. He'll meet me there.

He wouldn't say where he's flying in from, though. You know how secretive he is."

"Well, that's good then, isn't it?"

"I don't know. I'm nervous. Who knows what those fuckers are up to."

"Have they sent you any more threats?"

"Three this week. Didn't you see my funeral wreath? I found it on my car leaving the office the other day. The flowers were fake. Cheap bastards. Though they did splurge for a ribbon. 'You will be missed.' Assholes. It's in the garage if you want to take a look."

"Damn. I still think you should talk to the police."

"What can they do that I haven't already done? They've been trying for years to catch these guys. So what makes you think they'll be successful now? Besides, they'd just get in my way."

"Maybe you're right, but we'll never know, will we?"

"It's for the best. Trust me."

"What about your parents? Any word from them?"

"They're safe, as far as I know."

"You'll have to speak to them sooner or later."

Footsteps descending the stairs saved me from having to continue that unwelcome conversation. Cooper pried often. Yet it was comforting to know somebody cared enough about me to ask questions.

Laura appeared in a short dress. She seemed to have an endless supply of short dresses. Maybe that was where all her money went.

For the last three days, she'd been trying to elicit my attention in any way she could. She would pretend to fix a strap on one heel and tantalize me, rubbing her calf and ankle. She would come into my office for documents that didn't exist. Or prance into the kitchen and peek into the fridge, walking away, saying, "Huh, I thought we had horseradish." And this morning, she caught me staring at her while she was biting into a strawberry, so she sucked on it for a few seconds, then pulled it away as though it had been stuck to her mouth. Her tongue extended and swept slowly across her upper lip. Thankfully, Cooper was busy with the sport's section and didn't look up.

"Hey, guys." She plopped onto the adjacent couch and propped an elbow on her thigh, her legs crossed, one foot dancing in the air.

"How was your date with that Josh guy?" said Cooper.

"First of all, it's Jake, not Josh. Secondly, the date went really well. It was nice. He's nice." She gave me a hard stare. "In fact—we have another date tomorrow night. He's taking me to some fancy restaurant I've never heard of."

"That sounds like a good pl—"

"Cancel it."

"And why would I do that?"

"Yeah, why?"

"Because. I have business out of town. I have a few meetings and a large presentation. So I'll need your assistance. I'll email you the flight information this evening."

Cooper shot me a look. Bringing Laura to Colombia would put her in danger. I knew that. But I couldn't let that dull fucker take her on another date.

"You can't be serious," said Cooper. "You can't possibly need her in Colombia?"

"Colombia! Holy crap. I've always wanted to go there."

"Don't worry, Coop. It's strictly for work. I'll have a lot of paperwork coming to me down there, and I'll need her help sorting through it. And I might need her to meet some clients on my behalf, too, because I'll be occupied."

"I hear what you're saying, man. But no, absolutely not. I don't like the idea of Laura in South America. I heard the cartels down there cut out people's tongues for fun."

"Coop, I promise you, it'll be fine. She won't leave the hotel. The meetings she'll take for me are in the hotel lounge. Other than that, she'll be safe in the room with a pile of paperwork."

"I don't like it." He stood, pulled his phone out of his pocket, and left the living room.

"Why do I suspect this impromptu trip is just a plan to stop me from going on a date with Jake?"

"Don't flatter yourself. Why wouldn't I want you to date Sanders?"

"Only you know the answer to that." On her feet, "Now, if you'll excuse me, I have some packing to do. How many days worth of clothes do I need?"

"Four days, at most."

"Won't it annoy you to have me around for that long?"

"You have no idea."

"You still need my brother's permission."

"Wait for it."

"Huh?"

"I just got off the phone with a friend of mine in Medillin. I'm told, as long as she doesn't leave the hotel grounds, she shouldn't be in any danger. He gave me the number of his brother. He owns a taxi service near the airport. Here. However, if anything happens to her—I will kill you."

8
Laura

The moment our jet landed in Colombia, I wanted to stay forever, at least more than four days. We had to wait an hour for the taxi Cooper had instructed us to use, but it was worth it. Marcos gave us the names of different sites as we passed them. He carried my luggage into the hotel's lobby, wouldn't accept Sebastian's tip, and kissed the back of my hand. He said to call him anytime if we needed anything during our stay.

"I'm going to grab us some ice for the mini bar."

"You come right back. No detours. Stop grinning like that. I'm serious, Laura."

The hotel made me feel like royalty. Luxurious to the max. It had a spa, a gym, shiny marble floors, and antique-looking lamps. I lost count of how many pools there were. One had an arched bridge, which I walked on. And there was a chair shaped like a clamshell. Ooh, I saw a parrot that looked like Tucan Sam. It hung about the pool area but didn't stray too far from its perch beside the bar where its owner Alejandro worked. He made me a Hurricane in a tall, wavy glass with an orange slice and an extra cherry. The parrot's name was Cal, and he told me I was pretty. Actually, he said, "Hubba, hubba," but I knew what he meant.

"Where have you been? I thought I told you to come right back."

"I know but this place is so big and beautiful. There's so much to look at."

"What if something had happened to you. Huh?"

"You worry too much. You know what you need? A break."

"A break from what?"

"Work, silly. Come on, we've been here all day, and you've been cooped up in this room. Ooh, I have an idea."

"No. Whatever it is—no."

"Let's go over to the beach and watch the sunset. Oh, don't give me that look. Sunsets don't have to be romantic. They're just beautiful. And how often do you get to see a sunset in South America?"

"Go away. On second thought, no. Stay right there and don't say another word."

Being quiet and staying put was hard enough, but watching him work with that worried look in his eyes was too much. I wouldn't stand for it.

"Nuh-uh. You need a break." I closed his laptop.

"Laura, stop. I have work to do." He tried to snatch the laptop from my hands. I pulled it out of his reach.

"You've worked enough for today, don't you think?"

"You're really starting to piss me off. What do you suggest I do instead?"

"How about the pool. Yeah, let's go for a swim."

"I don't swim."

"You were in the Navy."

"Were, Laura. Were. I'm retired."

"Just this once?" I batted my lashes and pouted.

"Fine. But I'm not getting in the pool."

"Whatever. You can watch me get wet." I let that sink in. "In the pool, I mean."

He shook the daze from his head. "Go on, get changed. In the bathroom, Laura, not out here."

I gave him a sarcastic, "Yes, boss," then went to the bathroom and slipped into a red two-piece he couldn't ignore. We'd see about him not getting into the pool.

You should've seen his face when I walked out of the bathroom. He looked hungry—if you know what I mean.

At the pool, I tossed my towel on the lounge chair beside Sebastian and, standing over him, propped my hands on my hips, waiting. But he wouldn't look up from his phone. He was purposely ignoring me. I was sure of it.

So I pretended to slip backward and threw myself into the pool, shrieking. "Help!" I splashed around, flailing my arms, twice coming up for a gasp of air.

He jumped into the pool and pulled me to its edge. He analyzed my face, waiting for me to regain my composure. We both had one hand on the pool's lip, facing one another, our faces inches apart. The sound of miniature waves crashing against the pool's walls nearly mimicked my breathing rhythm. Even faking drowning takes a lot out of you.

"Are you okay?"

I couldn't control myself. My lips blubbered as laughter forced its way out.

For a second, he looked confused. "You little monster. You did that on purpose, didn't you?"

"I had to get you in the pool, somehow." I smirked.

"You are something else." He grabbed my hand and pulled me closer to him. The water shifted. His hands settled on my hips. I shivered. The scent of chlorine was strong. I hadn't noticed it until then. His fingertips ran along the sides of my upper legs. He grazed my inner thighs. My heart tickled. His hands moved upward and outlined my bikini's bottom from front to back. He plucked the strings, caressed my ass, and gave my cheeks a manly squeeze. Then he thrust his pelvis and pulled me against him.

What the fuck was happening?

"You drive me crazy, Laura. I don't know what to do with you."

One of his hands crawled between my legs from behind. He snuck a finger beneath my bikini and lightly rubbed my lips. My head fell back. I saw stars. I briefly wondered whether anybody might come for an after-dinner swim and catch us doing whatever it was we were doing.

Palm trees rustled in the twilight. His hand struggled to reach farther. But it didn't stop him from trying. His finger inched its way up and hooked into me. I winced, sucking air through my teeth.

His hand pulled away. Where'd it go? Put it back, damnit. Put it back now. "I wanted to rip this bikini off you the moment I saw you in it." Put that fucking hand back.

He grabbed my neck by the nape. "You're everywhere. I can't get you out of my fucking head." His thumb pressed hard against my neck's side. "You're all I hear, all I smell, and all I see." Pause. "You're all I fucking think about." He looked angry, fuming. It was so hot. "And you wanna know what goes on in my mind whenever I see you?" He yanked my head toward him, his grip tightening slightly. Then his nose swept upward, brushing my cheek, inhaling intensely. "Answer me, Laura."

I shook my head.

"Use your words."

"I-I—I don't know."

"All that runs through my mind . . . look at me when I'm talking to you. For fuck's sake, Laura. Pay attention—all that runs through my mind when I see you is how badly I want to tie you to my bedposts and fuck you till we're both dry and raw. Like the first time you walked into my office . . . ooh . . . I couldn't stop imagining you bent over my desk with that skimpy sundress pulled up over your back. I could almost feel your ass cheeks slamming into my thrusts—that's how much I thought about it."

"Sebastian . . ."

"You'd like that, wouldn't you?"

"I . . ."

"Speak up, Laura. Do you want me to fuck you?"

"Your—your hand—you're hurting me."

His phone rang. I'd forgotten we were in the pool, in Colombia, on Earth. Piece by piece, the world put itself back together: a palm tree there, a lounge chair there. Stars appeared one by one as though God struggled with their switches. I heard waves and smelled salt. The breeze's breath kissed my forehead.

Sebastian's eyes crept back into his head as it slowly retreated. "Fuck. This shouldn't have happened. Forgive me, Laura. I don't know what I was thinking." He sniffed the air and pushed back his wet hair. He hopped out of the pool. His shorts left a trail of water from the pool to the chairs. "I have to take this. I'll be in the room."

A black cat rushed by, leaving paw prints on the concrete.

Silence.

Through a chaotic mix of desire and shock, I'd lost my hearing, so it seemed. Now what was I supposed to do? I'd forgotten how to get out of a pool. I couldn't pull myself up over the edge. I'd tried. Had I always been this weak? I searched for stairs but wound up in the deep end, treading water for long enough to learn time only moves when you're present.

I couldn't remember getting out of the pool or walking to the bar. I could've murdered somebody in my travels, and I wouldn't have known. The cherry in my Pina Colada was flavorless. The bar was busy, but the people, the glassware, the mini umbrellas, and the entire scene all blurred together. Sounds were muffled and distant. I could still feel Sebastian's thumb pressing into my neck. My Pina Colada tasted like crushed ice. I wanted him to put his hand back. Why didn't he put his hand back?

"Laura, sweetheart. You okay?"

"Huh?"

"We're closing up soon. I take it you don't need another drink?"

It took me a few blinks and a shake of the head. "Um, no-no, I'm fine, Alejandro. Thanks for asking. What, uh . . . how much do I owe you? What? Have I already paid? No. Really, I'm fine. Thank you. I will. You too." My knees buckled while getting off the stool. I turned around. "Hey—Alejandro? How many have I had? Huh? Drinks—how many drinks have I had?"

"Just that one, Miss Laura. One sip. I only saw you take one sip. Was something wrong with it?"

"No, everything was great. The drink was delicious. I'm just . . . it's been a long day. I'm tired. You know?"

"Well then, get some rest. We'll see you tomorrow, yeah?"

"Tomorrow. That sounds nice."

I wandered, punch-drunk, drifting through a labyrinth of emotions I could not name or place. I had a song stuck in my head. Something in Spanish. It moved me. And I walked aimlessly about the hotel and hummed, running my fingers against a wall, dancing in my head. I might've twirled. Or maybe I imagined that because I'd always loved how a dress delicately rises with a spin, floats, and falls. I thought of that. I know I did. Then I outstretched my arms like airplane wings and wished. For nothing and everything, I wished.

And the door to the room appeared. Had I come here on my own? Had I consciously found the room, or was it an accident? I wanted to open it, just pull the handle down and push the door forward. Instead, I stared at the knob. The knob became a hand. The hand became a knob. I heard a sob coming from the room behind me. Glass shattered. Somebody told somebody they were no fucking good. That hand. The door. My neck, I reached across my body and touched it. I felt something. The door opened.

"What the fuck are you doing out here?"

"I was just, uh—"

"I heard shouting. I came out here to to tell somebody to shut the fuck up and found you standing here. Why do you look like a lost puppy?"

"Too much sun today. I think. And I had a drink. It was strong. I'm okay."

"If you say so."

I sat on my bed, my back against the wall, and watched him type. I studied his hands. Was it the right or the left? He would grunt every few minutes and massage the back of his neck. He was hunched over the keyboard, pecking. Every so often, he'd wriggle his nose. He had thick wrists. Black hairs. He wasn't hairy. He just had hair, the right amount of hair. This may not sound interesting to you, but I could've sat there and watched him type until my last breath, hungry and tired, a prisoner of my own body, my own doing, just watching a man type. Gasp. The end. Roll credits. Fucking heaven.

"Strip."

"Wuh-what?"

"You heard me. Strip. I want you to strip. Do you understand? Good. Do it.... Now."

I half-nodded. My chin seemed too heavy to raise my head.

"Laura." Twice he clapped. "I won't ask again. Take off your clothes, or I'll tear them off your body."

I did not move. He could do with me as he pleased.

"Fine. Have it your way."

Maybe I was being dramatic. Maybe I was so full of lust and wonder, so ecstatic from the euphoria of it all, that I chose to be a spectator of my own life. Maybe this was all a dream, and I would soon awaken in bed with my underwear cockeyed, his name on my lips, and a phantom bruise on my neck. But the way he pushed aside his laptop and jolted out of his seat, slowing to a crawl near the bed, creeping onto the mattress as though I were his prey—it felt real.

On all fours, he prowled toward me. I did not move, except when he grabbed my dress by the neck and tore it in half. Then I missed a breath, and my body jerked. I shrieked.

When had I put on a dress?

"I warned you." He yanked the dress from under me and tossed it. "No more games, Laura. I'm going to fuck you. Nod if you understand. Good." Sliding my underwear down my legs, he was gentle. The hair on his knuckles tickled. But I already had goosebumps.

He petted my hair, wrapped it around his hand, and yanked. My chin pointed toward the ceiling. My vocal cords stretched so tight that I couldn't utter a sound.

"Laura—I'm going to ask you a simple question. What happens next depends on your response." He tugged my hair. I thought my neck might snap in half. "Laura. Have you ever used a safe word?"

I went cross-eyed, peering at him over my nose. He hoisted himself up, his head hovering over my face. He released my hair, grabbed my chin, and squeezed my jaw. "Do you know what a safe word is used for?"

"Uh-huh."

"Good. Because I'm going to do things to you that I highly doubt anybody has ever done to you. Now choose your safe word."

"Lilac." I was awake. Coherent. The haze had cleared. You may wonder what happened to the sweet and bouncy Laura from twelve hours ago. I'll tell you. She died in that pool.

I knew whatever happened in this room wouldn't kill me, that the pain would enhance the pleasure, and that I would be grateful, eternally his. And later, tomorrow or next week, home or dreaming, till death did its part, his hand would be my hand.

"Lilac. I like that. It suits you." He removed his shirt and pants and went to the chair where he'd been typing earlier. His dick looked as if it would burst through his briefs. "Get over here. There ya go. That's a good girl. Now lay your stomach over my legs. Ass up. Don't make me work for it. Or it'll hurt worse. Got it."

A drop of dried blood on the cream-colored carpet was my focal point.

SLAP.

That hand. It had to be.

"That stunt in the pool."

SLAP.

My body jerked forward.

"Never again. You hear me?"

SLAP.

Fire. I felt fire.

"You've been playing games with me for too long."

SLAP.

My tits hung off his leg and jounced.

"No more fucking around."

SLAP.

The old Laura wouldn't like this.

"From now on, you do as I say. I fucking own you."

SLAP.

I heard it but didn't feel it.

"You don't like it, just say the word."

SLAP.

The old Laura would cry.

"Are those tears? Look at me when I'm talking to you. Aww . . . is this too much for you?"

SLAP.

The new Laura wanted more.

"I want to hear you say it. Tell me—who's in charge here?"

SLAP.

"You are."

No, I'd never experienced anything like this. I had no idea what would happen next, and I didn't care. The eroticism entangled with the pain bred a pleasure incomparable to sex alone. Being naked and numb with marvelous hurt spun me. My head whirled. My pussy ached with the yearning of a thousand forty-year-old virgins.

SLAP.

"Wake up. I'm just getting started."

He squirmed a bit, rubbing his hard dick against my belly.

"Up."

I stood, my knees shaky. The sting radiated from my ass to my thighs. My entire body pulsed.

"Turn around."

He stroked my ass, caressing each cheek as if he were shaping pottery. "It's beautiful. Red and pink and—what do you think, Laura? How does it feel?"

"Is that all you got?"

"Alright then. Get on the bed."

Something wet on my cheek, I wiped it.

"Now."

I climbed onto the bed. The anticipation of what might come next, the unknowing, pitter-pattered my heart. I sniffled and wiped my nose.

He went to the closet and returned with a leather belt. He stood at the bed's foot, folded the belt in half, and snapped it. I knew it was coming, yet I felt that snap echo in my bones. I'd never felt so naked, sitting there, my legs apart. I put my arms behind me to prop me up and keep the weight off my ass.

He kneeled on the bed. "Give me your hands." He wrapped the belt around my wrists. "There's nothing to tie you to, so this will have to do." I could wiggle my wrists but couldn't break free. He gave me a slight shove. I fell back. I put my tied hands above my head. My knuckles scraped the wall. He pushed my legs farther apart. Then he stood tall on his knees and pulled out his cock. His balls swayed against his briefs.

"I'm going to enjoy this." He stroked his cock, slowly. "Look at you—you're so fucking beautiful." His wrist bent with each stroke. He had a practiced flourish, went steady, and then fast.

"I can't take it, Sebastian. Are you going to fuck me or what? This is torture."

With one hand, he grabbed my face, giving me fish lips. "Did I tell you to talk? Be quiet. Your time will come." He lightly slapped my cheek. "Patience." His hand reached behind him. He slipped a finger or three inside my pussy. In and out. In and out. He licked his fingertips, shoved his fingers in his mouth, and sucked on them. "Damn—you taste good. You want a taste? I know you do."

I nodded, biting my tongue's tip. He put his fingers in my mouth. I raised my head off the pillow as much as possible, trying to swallow his hand. That hand. When he went to pull his fingers out, I bit down on them.

"You wanna play rough, huh?" He pulled me up by the hair. I'd forgotten how much my ass hurt. Sitting on it was only painful until he put his cock in my mouth. He held the back of my head and shoved my face against him while making short thrusts. My tied hands rested between my legs. My forearms got wet.

"Hey now, you're not going to cough up a hairball, are you?" Somehow, he pushed his cock deeper into my mouth. It was so fucking big. I tried to work my tongue but failed. His cock took up every inch of space. I dragged my teeth as gently as possible. My jaw couldn't open any farther. And breathing through my nose was difficult because every other second, it was pushed into his stomach. I kept gagging. He kept fucking my mouth. I loved it. How he roughly handled me and didn't treat me like some delicate princess was everything I didn't know I craved.

He pulled his cock out of my mouth, still clenching my hair. He dragged his tongue up my neck and kissed me. His stubble scratched my face. He shoved me back. Then his mouth traveled my body. He sucked on my nipples, kissed my hips, licked my navel, my clit, his fingers inside me, a hand clenching my left breast. My eyes twitched and rolled back to peek at my thoughts. He did so many things at once. So many feelings rushed through me, prickling my skin. I tingled. I wanted more.

He glared at me. My stomach heaved and blocked my view of his mouth with each rise. His nose glistened. "Turn over." He walked across the room and rummaged through his suitcase. "Get on all fours."

I glanced over my shoulder and saw him squirt something into his palm. He dipped a finger into it. "You remember your safe word?"

I nodded.

"Say it Laura. I need to hear you say the word."

Slowly and seriously, "Lilac." My face turned the color of what I imagined my ass was. Licking my lips, I could still taste myself.

"Good. If you want me to stop, just say the word. And I'll stop."

"Wait, what are. . . ."

"Shh...." He rubbed lube on my asshole. It was cold. A chill tip-toed up my spine. "Relax. You hear me? I need you to relax. The tenser you are, the more it'll hurt. Stay still. Understand?"

Was I for real about to have a dick in my *oww*.... I balled up the comforter in my fists. The head of his fat cock scraped its way farther in. My eyes squinted. He pushed more of it in. I hissed through clenched teeth. Somewhere in the mix was a moan. I was certain he'd torn my asshole. My mouth gaped so wide a sparrow could've flown out of it.

"Are you ready?"

I shook my head. He went slow. It was the most satisfying pain I'd ever felt. Three gentle thrusts and my body was ready to collapse into itself and explode. Holding my hips, his thrusts quickened. My body jerked. All my weight was supported weakly by my forearms. The belt dug into my wrists. My back was arched, my head low. I made noises, noises I can't explain. I'd never made or heard them. They were like moans but with subtle squeaks and deep groans, a mixture of sounds fit for a steamy symphony.

With his cock stretching my asshole wide, I could feel every inch of that beast, even the blood rushing through its veins. I was amazed. The pain was intense. I wanted to say something, talk dirty, or tell him how remarkable it all was, that I would never forget it. But I couldn't muster the air required to speak because I was so stuffed with cock.

Then he reached a hand around and massaged my clit. He rubbed my pussy from top to bottom, slowly dragging his fingers between my lips, pressing a bit, then back to my clit, rubbing and pushing, all the while thrusting, fucking my asshole. My face was squished against the mattress, my tied hands between my breasts. The pain had disappeared or was overshadowed by the cruel pleasure. I felt a premature nostalgia shaping, enhancing the euphoria but adding a dash of sadness.

"Sebastian, I'm going to come."

"Not yet. Now that I've claimed you, I need the rest." When he pulled out his dick, I was immensely relieved and upset. But I could breathe again.

He flipped me on my back and ran his hands up and down my legs. Then he pushed them out of his way. His briefs were still on, lowered just enough for his cock and balls to move freely.

He swept the head of his dick against my clit, skirted my lips, and patted my clit. "Is this what you want, Laura?" He stroked himself.

He forcefully shoved it in, slamming it into me. His energy passed to me and spread to my fingertips. It was a numbness rich with vitality. And he fucked me. He held onto my hips and fucked me hard. He would pull slowly back until the head of his cock was nearly out, then quickly thrust and smash into me. I swear I could feel his cock reach my throat.

He leaned over me, placing his palms on either side of my head, and kissed me. Then he slowly rebuilt his speed, his thrusts shortening with my breath.

"I'm gonna come. I can't hold it any longer. Fuck me. Fuck me harder. I never want it to end."

And then we came. He shot his load inside me. I felt the spurts. Then he pulled his cock out and stroked the last drops onto my stomach. The bottom of my ass was wet. My orgasm was unlike any orgasm anybody had ever had. It must've been. If somebody had had an orgasm like this before, they would have screamed about it from rooftops and posted it on Youtube or something. And I would've known this was possible. Right? I mean—what the fuck just happened?

He half-laid on top of me, smothering his sticky come against our stomachs. He petted my head. "You're such a good girl. I'm proud of you." He reached down between us and touched my pussy. I trembled and moaned. To say I was sensitive would be an understatement. I was raw and fragile. He brought the hand back up with a dab of his come on a fingertip. I licked it off. Then I sucked on his finger until my mouth hurt. He kissed me.

He went to the bathroom and returned with a wet washcloth. "I'm going to clean you up. You did so good, baby. I never thought you'd be able to handle all that."

As he cleaned me up, tenderly wiping my pussy and ass, I said, "I've never had sex like that. Never have I even thought about sex in that way. The things I felt, the things you did to me, I mean...."

"This is what I was scared of Laura. I knew you couldn't handle it."

"No. I loved it. Every ache and pain, every sting and slap, every tear and lost breath—I loved every fuckin' second of it."

He put his cock back in his briefs and smiled, pleased with himself.

9

Laura

The bed shook me awake. Sebastian rocked on his back, flailing his elbows and kicking his feet, mumbling. "Murray—no, I didn't . . . stop . . . it wasn't like . . . I tried to . . . don't do . . . I'm sorry." He rambled other sounds like words but nothing noteworthy or understandable. I hesitated to wake him, but once he started screaming, I tapped his shoulder.

He shouted, "It wasn't my fire." But he wasn't talking to me. I shook his shoulder, and he pulled it away. I stared at the muscles in his back, unable to decide what to do next. Was I crossing a boundary?

"Murray, you don't have . . . Dobbs, tell him he. . . ."

"Sebastian." I pushed his shoulder a few times. "Sebastian. Wake up." He swung an elbow at me, turning into it. He stopped, his body twisted, and looked behind me, not at me. Sweat seeped from the creases on his forehead. His eyelashes fluttered. The moonlight slashing through the blinds banded his face. He whipped around and untwisted his body, sprang up, and scooted back, away from me. "What the fuck are you doing?"

"Are you okay? You looked like you were—"

"I'm fine. Don't worry about it."

"Yeah, but... you were just—"

"I said I'm fine. Leave it alone, will ya." He went to the dresser and switched on a lamp. "Fuck, Laura. How many times do I have to tell you—know your place. You're my assistant, remember? You assist me. If I need an email written or a glass of fuckin' water, I'll let you know. Otherwise, keep your mouth shut."

"Are you really going to stand there and tell me I'm just your assistant after what we did tonight? Unless, I don't know, maybe you fuck all your assistants in the ass. Is that why they all leave you—because you fuck them in the ass and then treat them like shit?"

"Wow. Listen to the mouth on you. Is this the new Laura? You get a little kink in your life and all of sudden you think you can talk to your boss like he's your pip-squeak cousin. I don't know whether to kiss you or fire you."

"Maybe you should—

"No. I don't want to hear it. No more fucking questions. I don't need your advice. And I won't let you pry into my affairs." He went into the bathroom. The slam of the door startled me.

I rolled leftward with a huff, discovered a few stars through the slits in the blinds, and shrank into sleep with a wish.

Daylight, it took me a few seconds to remember where I was. You know the feeling. I recognized the room, remembered I was in Colombia, with Sebastian, and the sex. But as my remembrances unfolded and my last memory before falling asleep resurfaced, my glee became melancholy. Until Sebastian exited the bathroom, turned the corner with his head down, his biceps glistening, and started to unwrap the towel around his waist.

But he quickly closed the towel and tucked a corner to make it stay. "H-hey ...good morning. I was starting to think you might sleep the day away."

"What—what was that?"

"Just a habit, I suppose. You walk into a room in the process of getting naked and somebody you weren't expecting to see you sees you, and your natural reaction is to cover up. Right? It's got nothing to do with you."

"No, no, I mean your leg. On your leg, there's a bandage on it. Did something happen while I was asleep?"

"Oh, that. It happened the night before we left. A boring story involving a steak knife and a bottle of scotch. Nothing to worry about. Room service should be here with your breakfast in about thirty minutes."

"Are you going somewhere?"

"I have a meeting at ten. I should be back before lunch. While I'm away, go over the packet beside my computer and familiarize yourself with the details of the product launch I'm preparing to present tonight. Type a brief summary, just the bullet points, and email them to me."

"What about you? You're not going to stay for breakfast?"

"No time." He picked up a brush from the dresser and ran it through his hair. He caught my reflection staring at him.

"What is it?"

"Last night, can we talk about it? I mean, you really had me worried."

"About what?"

"In your sleep, you . . . you seemed to be in a lot of pain."

"It was just a nightmare. Everybody gets them. Not a big deal."

"Not a big deal. That wasn't your average, run-of-the-mill nightmare, Sebastian, and you know it. People don't scream in their sleep for no reason. Please, you can talk to—"

"Enough. I can't give you what you want. This has already gone too far. I'm going crazy over here—questioning my morals—discovering emotions I never knew existed. I'm losing my fucking mind. You already live in my thoughts; I won't share them, too. I can't give you whatever cutesy affectionate connection it is you seek. So stop trying."

"Why? Why can't you open up and talk to me like a real human being? What's stopping you? Are you worried it might ruin your image? Is it our ages? Or because I'm Cooper's little sister?"

"I just . . . I just can't. It's too dangerous."

"Dangerous? That doesn't make any sense. There's nothing dangerous about me."

"It's not you I'm worried about. You shouldn't even be here. . . . No, I can't. I've said too much already. Bringing you here was a mistake. And last night never should've happened. It can't happen again. Understand? Nothing can or will ever happen between us again. End of story."

10
Sebastian

Waiting for Matt to find his tongue, I stirred my whisky, then let the ice do its thing.

"They've been investigating a woman named Laura Anderson. She's your assistant, right?"

"What? Why the fuck would they investigate her?"

"Maybe they think she can get access to the thumb drive. They could blackmail her or offer her a ton of money, which, if she hates you, and she probably does, she wouldn't think twice about taking a bribe. Unless she's a mormon. Is she a mormon?"

"How the fuck would I know? Just tell me what they have on her."

"Her past, her present, her family, everything about her. Now, I would tell you not to mention any of this to her—because tipping her off would make matters worse—but, knowing you, you'll probably have a new assistant by lunch, making their investigation useless."

"Then I'll fire her."

"Whoa, slow down. Put your phone away. You do that, and it'll tip them off. They'll know that you know what they're up to, and then who knows what they'll do."

"Great. Well, I should tell her, right? I mean, I should say something, warn her somehow, and get ahead of this thing."

"Absolutely not. Right now, you say nothing. Tell her only what she needs to know. Mention none of this unless her life becomes in danger."

"Her life is in danger, damnit."

"Immediate danger. And anyway, why do you care so much about what happens to your assistant? Shit—you're not fucking her, are you?"

"She's Cooper's little sister. . . . No, that's a no. I'm not going to fuck my best friend's sister, let alone some measly assistant." I drained my whisky. "Anything else?"

"You might want to order another one."

I signaled the bartender for a second round.

"So . . . how do I put this delicately . . . you have a rat in your company."

"You're shitten me? How the fuck did those bastards sneak a rat into Anderson Tech?"

"Not including board members and executives, there are over a thousand employees at Anderson Tech. If I had to guess, I would say at least one out of every twenty people are ripe for snitching. Some people get off on it. It's an adrenaline thing."

"Yeah-yeah, whatever. Are you going to tell me anything useful? Like how to smoke out the rat and uncover the information he's handed over."

"I'm working on that. For now, just sit tight. And be careful at work. Don't talk to anybody, especially not your assistant."

"For the last time, I have no desire to talk to my assistant. She's as useless as they come. I forgot she existed until you'd mentioned her name."

"Good to see some things haven't changed. As soon as I know more, I'll contact you."

"How am I supposed to know who to trust?"

"That's easy. Trust nobody."

Back in the room, Laura was sitting at the table, typing on her laptop, a pillow under her ass.

"That was quicker than I'd expected. Do you wanna grab some lunch soon? I've been dying to try that restaurant downstairs."

"I can't. I have to prepare for tonight's presentation. I'll just order in."

"Alright, let me know if you need anything. I'll be downstairs."

"Okay.... Wait! Don't go anywhere."

"Oh, come on. I promise I won't leave the hotel. I'll go straight to the restaurant and come right back. I won't even use the restroom while I'm away."

"That came out wrong. It's just—I changed my mind. But let's eat here, in the room. I can take a little break for lunch. I just don't have time to go downstairs and then wait to order and wait for the food and all that."

"Sure. That's fine, though I was really looking forward to eating there. But how can I pass up an opportunity to have lunch with you, especially when you're being nice?"

"Right. You look over the menu and call it in. I'll have a sandwhich, turkey, if they have it. I'm not picky. But you must allow me to work. No disturbances."

"You won't hear a peep from me. I'll just busy myself with some emails. God knows I never run out of those."

I had a comment for that but pretended not to hear her. All that mattered was she didn't leave my sight, that and readying myself for tonight. True to her word, she remained quiet, sitting against the wall on the bed, legs crossed, her laptop on her lap, and her bare feet swaying to what I assumed was a song stuck in her head. She had a rhythm. From the corner of my eye, her feet waving about distracted me. A freckle on her left ankle drew more of my attention and brought my eyes to her calves, her knees, and a tease of her thighs. It was madness. I had to focus.

She ate her BLT with the grace of a toddler. She chewed with her mouth open and talked while chewing. How had I not noticed this before? Had I seen her eat? You'd think it would be a turn-off, yet somehow, she still looked sexy. The power of pussy, I suppose. She was too busy stuffing her face to care that I only took two bites of my Turkey Club and went back to work.

I didn't tell her she had mayonnaise on her chin until we started getting ready for the dinner being held for the presentation. She wore a sultry black dress with a thigh-high slit, her hair wrapped in a sleek ponytail. She was so effortlessly beautiful. I backed her against the door, slipped my hand under her dress, and kissed her—except that didn't happen. I behaved myself, much to my disappointment.

"We must be early. There's hardly anybody here."

"That's good. Clients hate arriving before you."

"FYI, you look really handsome tonight, as usual."

"Not half as stunning as you do." It was a slip of the tongue. I couldn't stop myself.

"Sebastian!" said a familiar voice.

I turned. "Maria, it's so nice to see you." She hugged me, kissed my cheek, reached up, and chucked me under the chin. Maria was old-money rich. Her earrings could put an entire class through college, and the surgeries had not helped her face. She was eighty-two and looked like a mangled seventy-year-old.

"Tell me about it. It's like you completely went off the grid." She chuckled. "Oh, and who is this cutie beside you, your new woman? I knew you liked them young, Sebastian, but this one looks like she's out past her curfew."

I winced internally, wishing for the ground to open up and swallow me whole. "This is Laura Anderson, and no, she's not my new woman. She's just my assistant."

Her face remained still as her jaw dropped. "Dear, I'm so terribly sorry for my jumping to conclusions like that. It's a habit, a bad one. It isn't intentional. I do mean well."

"It's okay, ma'am. It's nice to meet you."

"And lovely to meet you, such a beauty. Ooh, I seemed to have lost my . . . Charles . . . Charles honey. Oh, there you are. Be a dear and fetch me a martini, will you? Yes, dear. We'll be right over here."

I cleared my throat. "Why don't we all sit while waiting for everyone else to show."

"Yes, please. My knees are about to give out any second."

As you might've imagined, Laura's face dimmed when I'd said she wasn't my woman. I didn't understand her disappointment. She had no reason to presume we were anything other than . . . well, you get the point. Still, it pained me to see her hurt by my comment. Keeping her at a distance while keeping her close would be a challenge.

11

Laura

What an asshole.

He could've said I wasn't his woman or girlfriend or whatever and left it at that. It was the truth, and I had no qualms with it. Nor was I troubled by him calling me his assistant. It was that one little word that set me off. You know the one: "just". I could've slapped him. I should have. Oh, "She's *just* my assistant." Dick.

I let it slide, though, and by letting it slide, I mean I didn't speak to him most of the evening unless I had to. He'd introduce me to clients and friends, and I would shake hands and smile and nod and turn away and sigh. Even if I had been in a decent mood, the night would've exhausted me. Still, I never said a word to him about his belittling comment. He knew I was angry. No need to get him all riled up when he was already so sensitive and wishy-washy.

Once back in the room, I went straight to bed—in my bed, not his—and for the remainder of the trip, I ignored my emotions and desires and focused on work. If he saw me as just his assistant, then I would *just be* his assistant. If that makes any sense. Of course, I'd hoped he'd buy me flowers, take me out, go dancing, or something special attached to an apology, so I could stop fighting my urges and act accordingly.

But no, not even a sorry or a good night. I should've known better, anyway. The most delightful words he'd told me during our last thirty-six hours in Colombia were: "The bathroom's free." And that was one hour prior to us leaving for the airport, where he didn't offer to help me with my luggage and let a door close before I'd crossed the threshold. Slam, right into my suitcase, "Oops, sorry, I thought you were right behind me." He was clearly preoccupied and hadn't the time to be either mean or nice to me. Which would've been fine had he at least acknowledged me once in a while.

Even on the airplane, he couldn't be bothered by me. He was on his laptop the entire flight. And when the flight attendant came around to take drink orders while I was banging around in the restroom, he forgot to order me the wine spritzer I'd asked him to get.

In his defense, he was in rough shape. His eyes were puffy and sagging and had dark circles around them. He hadn't shaved since the morning of the presentation and nearly had a full-grown beard. I don't normally like bearded men, but Sebastian could've let it grow another five inches and still been hotter than Hell.

Once we landed and after I'd chased Sebastian through the airport because he seemed to be in a rush to get somewhere, he dropped me off at home, saying, "I've gotta head to the office. I've got a lot of stuff to catch up on. I'll see you tomorrow."

Umm, okay.

I already missed Colombia, but I was glad the trip was over. Everything just got quiet and weird after that dinner and presentation, and I still had no clue whether it was a success.

I tossed my suitcase onto my bed and sat on its edge for a breath. Then Bianca texted me, wanting me to spend the weekend at her apartment. A fantastic idea, I thought. I needed the girl time. I grabbed my suitcase and left. I could do laundry at her place.

I stopped at an Aldi and bought Smartfood, Combos, and Twizzlers. I paid in cash, dropped a dollar in the plastic jar, and wondered if my money would really be used to help somebody's dog get a hip replacement. But it was too late. You can't take it back once it's in.

I set the bag of munchies on the passenger seat. And while rummaging through my purse for my keys, something touched the back of my head. It was cold and felt like metal. I smelled body odor and Drakkar Noir. "Shh . . . stay quiet and I won't hurt you. Scream—you die."

"P-please, don't kill me. There's some money in my purse. Take it. Take whatever you want, just don't kill me."

He cackled. "I don't need your money, Laura. Your loverboy has something that belongs to me. And I want it back."

"Loverboy?"

"Don't play dumb with me. I'm not a patient man, and I won't hesitate to splatter your brains all over this windshield." He tapped my head with the gun's barrel. "I know you and Sebastian Delarossi are messing around. I have pictures. Yeeess. I was in Colombia, watching your every move. Now, I have reason to believe you might know where Sebastian is hiding a certain thumb drive. It's very special to me. And I will do anything to get it back, including killing you and your entire family, starting with Cooper. That way, you can watch."

"I swear I have no idea what you're talking about. Sebastian doesn't tell me anything. The man is completely closed off. I know nothing about him other than he was in the Navy and works at Anderson Tech. That's it. That's all I know."

The gun shifted against my head as he glanced left, then right. In the rearview, I saw his forehead and eyes. They were a beautiful light blue with a marble-like tint and glossy with pin-drop pupils. Just below his eyes was the seam of a black cloth or mask.

"Yes, Sebastian is a difficult man. I understand your dilemma, but . . . you have no choice. I don't care how you do it. Just get it done. You have one week.

I'll text you in six days to tell you where to meet me. Have I made myself clear? Good."

He reached around me while leaning against the back of my seat and shoved the gun's barrel upside my chin. He whispered in my ear. "If you tell anyone about this or go to the police, I *will* kill you. And after a week, if I don't have that thumb drive in my hands, I'll kill one of your relatives each day until I have it. And if I run out of relatives, I'll start killing your friends. Do you understand?" He moved away and leaned against the backseat. His entire masked face was now visible in the rearview. He stared at me through the mirror for an uncomfortably long time without moving or blinking. "One week," he said, as if I needed the reminder. He cracked the door open, stopped, and said, "Oh, and enjoy your weekend with Bianca. I hear she's made Jello shots. Should be fun." He winked and was gone.

I had to tell Sebastian. Right? I mean—what the fuck? I couldn't even drive. I was shaking hysterically. I ordered an Uber, and on the way to Anderson Tech, the scent of Drakkar Noir lingered. It must've been on his wrists and transferred to my dress. As if that scent wasn't horrible enough, now whenever I caught a whiff of it, I would remember having a gun pointed at my head. I would burn this dress the first chance I got. I couldn't stop shaking. My breaths were short and rapid. The Uber driver wanted to know whether I liked the song on the radio because he would change it if it wasn't my thing. What song? Goddamnit, what just happened? I pinched myself. Shit.

In the elevator, I pretended to breathe into a paper bag and waved the front of my dress. I felt claustrophobic, was burning hot, and seemed to be shrinking.

"Hey, beautiful. I feel like I haven't seen you in forever."

"Not now, Jake. Is Sebastian in his office?"

"Yeah, but . . . I wouldn't go in there."

"And why not?"

Jake scratched the back of his neck. "He is . . . it's just . . . he's a little occupied at the moment."

"What in the hell is that supposed to mean?"

"He has a visitor. And I don't think he would want to be interrupted."

"A visitor? Cut the crap, Jake. What's going—" Sebastian's office door opened.

A ditzy giggle preceded Viviane walking out of Sebastian's office, her hair all tangled. Some buttons of her shirt were undone. Sebastian followed her out, his tie cockeyed, hair disheveled.

Tears, uncontrollable tears that stung like acid, trickled down my cheeks. Knowing he'd fucked Vivianne again was hard enough, but that he was getting off while I had a gun pointed at my head for something he did—it enraged me.

"Oh, hey, Laura. I didn't expect to see you here." Buttoning her shirt, she looked at Sebastian. "Didn't you say she was at home?"

"Laura, I know what you think. It's not what this looks like—"

"Save it, Sebastian." I turned and ran.

"Laura! C'mon, come back. I can explain."

12

Laura

What an asshole.

Did I already say that? My mind was a mess. I couldn't stop thinking about Vivianne's unbuttoned shirt. A bruise irritated the back of my head. Drakkar Noir scented my oxygen. Gross. I would've rathered the man's body odor had clung to me instead of that nasty crap. And how would I tell Sebastian about the thumb drive and the one week I had before everybody I knew was killed? Like, there must've been thousands of thumb drives in that building alone, never mind in our house. Cooper had them laying around everywhere, ditto with Sebastian. None of them were labeled. Meanwhile, tick-tock went the clock on my family's lives. But I couldn't just call Sebastian and drop such heavy information on him, not without talking to him. Yes, I was avoiding him. And it was hard. He'd been calling and texting me from his office nonstop all night. Fucking Vivianne.

So I went to Cooper and told him. I begged him not to report it to the police, and he obliged. Perhaps because his life was also on the line. Or maybe because a police report would have interfered with the overnight trip that he was packing for and being secretive about.

Cooper would tell Sebastian. That was the plan. He said it was imperative Sebastian and I talk. He had to hear it from me, Coop said. Which made sense, I guess. Still, I had no desire to speak to that pig. Yeah, I said "pig." I was really pissed off. Even a hot guy can be a pig. You must know this.

The emotional distress upsetting me was as real and scary as the threat against my life. And what better way to distract me from my impending death and my bleeding heart than to head to the club with Bianca and get tipsy on overpriced cocktails bought by men wearing cheap chains who likely live in their mothers' basements and refer to each other as "bro", only to have them sloppily attempt to grind our thighs while pretending we can't see their little erections nudging out the zippers of their stonewashed jeans. I think that about sums it up. I was really looking forward to it.

Then I was half-blinded by strobe lights and Cosmos. The room did its own dance.

"B! Hey—B! Bee-anc-AH. Hey, I need to use the restroom. Be back in a minute. Don't go anywhere. I said—don't go anywhere. Stay right here. I said—never mind."

The hallway walls leading me to the bathroom were sticky. Blacklights lined the ceiling. The floor seemed slanted.

A barefooted woman whose toenails were painted red banged on the stall door. "Occupied," I said. She banged on it again. "Hey, somebody's in here. Go away."

A faucet gushed water. The woman groaned and mumbled. "Stupid motherfuckers." At least, that's how I remember it. She could've said cheese sticks, for all I know. Then she slurred incoherent words, followed by, "I'll show those cocksuckers."

I was afraid to leave the stall. I didn't flush the toilet until I heard the door squeak open and shut. Still, I was nervous. What if, instead of her leaving, somebody new had entered the women's room? But I couldn't stay in the bathroom all night. What was happening to me?

I opened the stall door, heard a squeak, and recoiled. Just as I was about to lock myself back in the stall, an imposter walked in. Sebastian. What fresh Hell was this?

How had he found me?

I steeled myself, said nothing, went to the sink, and washed my hands.

"Why, hello to you, too, Laura. You look like you're having a good night."

"Go away, will ya?" I tore off a brown paper towel, swiped my hand beneath the dispenser, and tore off the next one, then the next one, and again, and so on.

"Laura, you're drunk as hell. Look at you, you can't even stand straight."

"Fuck (hiccup) off. What are you doing in here anyway? This is the *woomen's* room."

"I had to see you. I'm concerned about you. I've been worrying all night. Cooper told me what happened. I'm sorry.

"Oh, please—you—worried about (hiccup) me. I doubt that."

"What're you talking about?"

"Nothing. Forget about it." I ripped off another paper towel. "You still haven't answered me. How'd you know where I (hiccup) was?"

"Cooper told me you were staying at Bianca's, so I contacted her. She told me you guys were here. Now tell me—why were you ignoring my calls?"

"Isn't it *obv-ious*? I don't want to see you, *or* talk to you."

"Goddamnit, Laura. You were held at gunpoint. That's not something you can just get drunk and sleep off. When were you going to tell me?"

"That was why I went to your office, to tell (hiccup) you. And maybe I would've gotten the chance had you not been fucking *Vivianne*."

"Is that what this is about? Jesus, Laura. Maybe that's how it looked to you, but I assure you, I did not fuck Vivianne tonight. And if you hadn't stormed off, you would already know this."

"As if I would believe *herrrr*you."

"For fuck's sake, listen to me: I did not sleep with her. She tried, but I pushed her away."

"What-ever."

"You should've told me about the gunman, Laura. This isn't a joke. Do you have any idea the danger you're in?"

"I'm alive (hiccup), aren't I?"

A woman wearing a shade of lipstick that I wouldn't dare wear clip-clopped into the bathroom without giving Sebastian a second look. He and I stared at one another. A mixture of angst and lust was what I saw in his eyes, though perhaps it was my reflection. We didn't move.

The woman exited a stall, washed her hands behind me, and left.

"We're leaving this place right now. And you're coming with me. Then you're going to tell me exactly what happened and what that man told you."

"I'm not going anywhere with the likes of *you*."

"Listen, I know you're mad at me. But I'm begging you. You're not safe here. I swear—I'll explain everything to you once we're home."

"Fine. I'll go. But only because I'm (hiccup), and these shoes are killing my feet."

He tried to hold my hand as we walked through the black-lighted hallway. "Thanks but no thanks. I can walk on myself." Then I missed a step and stumbled forward, nearly falling on my face.

Sebastian caught me. "You're so stubborn." He shook his head. I allowed him to hold my hand. "We're taking Bianca with us. Where is she?"

Bianca was a treat. "You can't boss me around in here. This isn't the fuckin' office, and I don't have to listen to you." Sebastian dragged her out of there, pulling her by the hand. She screamed and shouted all the way to the car, where she tired out and fell silent.

Sebastian helped us both into the backseat. Bianca was snoring before he even shut my door. The way her body was half-laid and -sat on its side, how her lips curled, her knees bunched up, she looked sad. Or was it my reflection in the window that looked sad?

13

Sebastian

It was all my fault. I was so focused on getting to the office and caring for myself that I neglected Laura's safety. She could've been injured, killed, or abducted. That she was alive and physically unharmed was not luck. The traffickers were using her to get the thumb drive, as Matt had warned they would, but how? I was eager to learn the gunman's instructions to Laura, though having her recount the incident would likely be an emotional task, one I would have to handle delicately.

She looked adorable, passed out in the backseat, her head against a window, still pouting. Bianca lay across the seat, her head beside Laura's ass, nearly sucking her thumb.

I almost felt bad for waking Bianca, except not really. Her head rose wearily. She tried to look everywhere at once, smacked her lips, and said, "Where am I?"

Laura awakened, hugged her friend, and lazily said goodbye.

"Why am I in the backseat?"

"You wanted to sit in the back with her. You can come up front if you want."

How had this happened? I'd not been this crazy about a female since Loose Lucy let me touch her developing breasts in her treehouse while playing spin the stick one gray afternoon after Sunday School. She wasn't as loose as her nickname portrayed, though. She drove me batty for a few weeks, leading me to believe I'd get another touch or be allowed to travel southward and explore new regions of her body. I was over her a few weeks after the breast incident. And I vowed never again to let a woman have control over me like that.

But Laura, unaware as she was, had me hooked. I couldn't look up from my desk or walk from point A to point B without thinking about her and those sleek legs.

Which was why I had difficulty paying attention to the road when driving us home. The dashboard's glow shined off her legs. She stared out her window, her arms crossed.

"So you're really not going to talk to me?"

"I have nothing to say to you."

I pulled the car into our house's garage. Parked on our right was her Camry. She stared at it.

"Before Cooper left town, he brought me to the Aldi, and I drove it home. I hope that's okay?"

"That was . . . that was very kind of you. You didn't have to do that."

"It's the least I could do. What happened earlier, the man who threatened you, I—I can't imagine how terrified you must've been. And if words could make you forget, I would spend the rest of my life talking to you, apologizing. I'm sorry, Laura."

"Can we just not talk about it right now. My head's starting to hurt a bit."

"Laura—please, just let me talk for a minute. I can't take back what happened to you. And make no mistake about it, I take full responsibility. It was one-hundred percent my fault. And I'll be eternally sorry for the pain and suffering this has caused you. Seriously. But these men . . . Laura, please, I'm trying to tell you something. These men, the ones who sent that man after you, they're not stick-up kids and purse-snatchers. They're worldwide. They have deep pockets. And in those pockets are senators and congressmen, governors, presidents, and prime ministers. Do you understand? This is serious. They will kill you just for talking to me. Now, I know you don't want to, and it will be difficult, but we must talk about this. I need to know what that man told you, word for word. His tone. His mannerisms. Did he have tattoos? If he sneezed, I want to know about it. I need every detail."

Damnit. She was crying.

"Hey." I lifted her chin. "It'll be okay. You have nothing to worry about. I won't let anything like that ever happen to you again. I promise."

Sullen and weak, her chin dipping, she said, "Okay."

"Laura, look at me, please. Everything is going to be fine. Believe me."

She wiped tears from her eyes, streaking her mascara. Then she hugged me with the strength of a wife seeing her husband off to war. I could've lived in her sad embrace until death did its thing. No, I didn't want her to be sad, not then or ever. But there was something to it, something that made me content, as if all the madness, internally and externally, had lost its spin. A calmness emerged within me. And then it hit me. It wasn't her sadness I basked in but that she needed me.

My entire life, nobody had ever needed me. Not like this. The concept was just as foreign to me as the feeling it awarded me. Sure, plenty of women had wanted me, which came with its own egotistical feeling that I'd grown used to. I thrived on it. Laura wanted me, and that was great. But she didn't need me, not until now. And the warmth of her needful arms transmitted a tranquility unequal to any emotion I'd ever encountered.

I didn't want the moment to end, but we couldn't stay in the car all night. "Laura." I pulled my cheek away from her head, signaling her to move. "We should get inside."

She stared intensely at me. I kissed her in my thoughts, lovingly, a slow-motion peck, the kind when the lips barely touch yet stay together with a held breath longer than your lungs would like. Because you don't fear dying when amid a kiss as passionate as the one I imagined while Laura's eyes begged me to kiss her.

But then I flinched. She said she was cold. I said I was hungry. I opened her door for her. We walked inside, holding hands as though walking through a gauntlet of lockers. She went into the living room. I went to the kitchen and tried to remember why I went into the kitchen.

I returned to the living room, a bottled water in hand, and found Laura asleep. I set the water on the coffee table, scooped her up, and carried her up the stairs. Her head wavered against my bicep. I walked slower. She groaned, murmurs almost forming words, yet nothing I could decode. As I cautiously placed her on her bed, her eyes opened. She silently watched me pull a blanket from the bed's foot and drape it over her. I lifted her head and adjusted her pillow.

Softly, she said, "That man . . . the one from—"

"Shh. It can wait." My face hovered over hers, a kiss away. "We'll talk about it first thing in the morning. Just get some rest. You've had a long day."

Her head lifted a little from the pillow, her face reaching for mine. She paused as if trying to read my mind before proceeding, then moved her head a pinch upward. I moved to meet her halfway but stopped. Her head collapsed onto the pillow. Suspense delayed the inevitable kiss. Just a peck, though our lips remained joined and still until exhaling broke the spell. Our faces peeled apart, yet they didn't go far. We smiled.

Then I kissed her without restraint, unthinking, and empty of intentions. My body moved as it pleased, guided not by me but as if by an unknown entity living inside me. I could feel, though, and I felt. Yet my senses were disordered. I couldn't recall how the blanket once covering her had fallen to the floor or who removed her underwear. But I knew her lips tasted of vodka and want. Her hands unbuckling my pants felt like freedom. I was so immersed in the moment that she had to grab my hand and put it up her dress, pressing it against her wet pussy, as if I'd forgotten what came next. With two fingers inside her, my thumb massaging her clit, I moved slowly, using short strokes. Her juices trickled down the back of my hand. Her moans traveled down my spine. My free hand grabbed her neck. I started to squeeze but stopped, pulling my hand away in favor of a breast.

My pants were on the floor. She was stroking my cock, underhanded. She pulled me closer, by the cock, gently enough. Then, as my cock tried to comprehend the wet warmth her pussy had blessed it with, she wrapped her arms around me and drew me closer. She kissed me. My hand grabbed her neck. I pulled it away in favor of a breast. I yanked her dress up and sucked on her nipples, nibbling here and there, licking everywhere. Her moans echoed through the room and caressed my ears.

My thrusts were compassionate, slow, and wonderful. Occasionally I'd linger when completely in, attempting to push my cock deeper inside her. Our pelvises almost created enough friction to start a fire. She would lift her ass a notch and push when I pushed, an intense collaboration in hopes of getting my cock to do magic tricks, to bend, grow, or stretch, anything as long as it reached new depths.

My hand squeezed her neck, lightly. Still, I pulled it way in favor of a breast. We kissed, a lot. I'd never kissed so much during sex. She played with her clit. I could take a hint. I thrust faster. Her moans rose an octave, the volume rising until they were one continuous moan. My face must've had the look of a boy unexpectedly walking into a brothel. Because I was confused, bewildered, befuddled, call it whatever you want. Who was I right now?

14

Sebastian

"While I was in the Navy, I discovered files containing information exposing a sex trafficking ring. Yes, I'm dead serious. The organization had documented every detail concerning their operations, locations, and hierarchy, including ledgers of pay offs and other off-the-books transactions, and they had everything stored in these files . . . Yeah, well I did. I tried, anyway. The police have been trying to bring these assholes down for years but nothing . . . I know. Well, last I heard, it had something to do with legal barriers and warrants, something about how the files were obtained or some bullshit. Most likely, they, the asshole traffickers, have cops and agents on the take. It's the only possible explanation."

"So, wait a second, is that what's on the thumb drive that that man asked me to find?"

"Yeah. We'll get to that. Coffee? . . . But there's more you need to know first. So—back when these files landed in my hands, I'd intended to turn them over to the authorities, like I said, but they threatened to kill me. Creamer? . . . No, not the authorities, the sex traffickers; they threatened me. Anyway, I refused to give the files to them, the drive. And just before I'd shipped out for another tour, they'd somehow planted explosives on the ship, which . . . well . . . two days at sea, and . . . boom. Everybody on board died but me. . . . Coast Guard. I don't know. Honestly, I barely remember. But somehow, I made it off that ship alive and survived five hours in the sea, though I often wish I hadn't."

"Jesus. . . ."

"No, Jesus wasn't there. But I would like to have a word with him. Anyway, to make matters worse, I was blamed for the fire and dishonorably discharged. No kidding. I handled none of this well. All those deaths, my shipmates, their blood was on my hands. I still believe that. Survivors guilt, I think it's called. It was too much. I hated myself. More than anything I wanted to . . . let's just say I had difficulty moving on. . . . That's what I'm trying to say. . . . No, that was it . . . I swear. Maybe that's enough history for the day."

"Sebastian, just tell me. Whatever it is I . . . I won't judge."

"You don't know that. But sure, what the hell. So, at one point . . . sorry, this is . . . I've never shared this with anyone. In fact, other than your brother, you're the first person I've opened up to about all this. That's not hard to believe, I know. But I think that says something about you and . . . about my level of comfortability around you. You know what I mean?"

"You're stalling."

"Right. Maybe I am. You sure you want to hear this? Okay, okay. So I was having a shit time of it, like I said, and I was drinking and starting fights at bars and all around just being a total shit bag. Every fight I got into, in the back of my fucked up head, I secretly hoped the other guy would just beat me dead or pull out a gun and put one through my skull. Don't do that. Don't make that face. Now I don't want to finish. Fine, fine. So basically I was just begging for the reaper to appear with his sickle and hood and drag me down to Hell where I thought I belonged. Maybe I do. Anyway, I wanted it all to end so badly that once . . . well, I suppose there's no nice way say it—I tried to commit suicide. Yes, it's awful and embarrassing, and I'm not proud of myself. But there you have it . . . huh? . . . Oh, Cooper found me and rushed me to the hospital.

This is why he's so protective of me and fears leaving me alone, which is why he sent you to be my assistant, to look after me."

"I—I don't know what to say. It's all so...."

"Fucked up."

"Yeah. No wonder you're always so—"

"Cold."

"I was going to say distant. You keep everybody an arm's length away. And you never—

"Talk."

"Would you stop that? I was going to say open up. And since we're on the subject, why did you tell me all this? You could have just as easily told me nothing and still done whatever it is you need to do to get those degenerates behind bars. Why tell somebody now? Why me?"

"Because I want you to know the depth of what you're involved in. And I care about you. I don't know what that means or even how to process it. But it's the truth. If only Cooper and I had thought about the danger we were putting you in when making you my assistant. We should've known better."

"Wait . . . you care about me?

"Okay, can we not dwell on that right now. I need you to tell me what happened in your car. Let's open that can of worms and see if we can avoid being killed before we start talking about anything I may or may not have said about you. Deal?"

"Fine. But I won't forget. I'll bug you if I have to."

"That's fine. Now...."

She told me everything, the man's mask, the barcode tattooed on the back of his left hand, his cold marble-blue eyes, his knowing Bianca's name, and even how she peed a little in her pants when first realizing he was in the car. I listened intently and tried to remain aware of my body language and tone, though I rarely spoke because I thought disrupting her narrative would only divert her attention and make it more difficult for her to continue. So I saved my questions, sipped my coffee, and nodded, occasionally reaching over a plate of half-eaten pancakes to rest a hand on top of hers, a touch of compassion, if you will.

We had six days, no plan, and were sitting still, caught in each other's gaze. She leaned in first. I followed. Then we simultaneously and slowly moved closer. The refrigerator's hum died. We paused, our lips a whisper away. Then the front door opened. And we hurriedly began cleaning the kitchen, busying ourselves in hopes of shedding our guilt and displaying a sense of normality.

Cooper walked into the kitchen, a strap over his shoulder. "Hey guys. What'd I miss?"

Laura and I, our hands in the sink, looked at one another for an answer and waited for somebody to speak.

15

Laura

"No, it's not a date. He's just been texting me like crazy and, I don't know, I feel like maybe I might've led him on and given him the wrong impression. . . . Because I don't want to date him. Oh, stop. . . . Because I'm not a big slut like you. I know he's sweet and handsome and well-mannered and everything that any sane woman would want in a man but . . . it's just . . . he's boring. Haven't I told you all this already? . . . Are you eating? . . . Because you chew like a horse and all that crunching in my ear is distracting. . . . Stop calling it a date. . . . Because he deserves an explanation. Besides, I've been locked up in this house for three days, and I could really use the fresh air. . . . It's hard to explain. . . . Okay, I can't tell you. How's that? . . . Whatever. . . . Tonight. I'm meeting him at that new restaurant on the corner of Ashbery and Bloom. I think it's French. . . . That's why I need to talk to him. . . . I don't know, nothing too revealing. I don't wanna send the wrong vibes. . . . For the hundredth time—it's not a date."

"What's not a date?"

"Shit, I gotta go. I'll call you tomorrow. Oh, shut up. Bye."

"Heyy . . . how long you been standing there?"

"Long enough to know what restaurant you won't be going to tonight."

"Oh, come on. If you know the restaurant, then you know it's not even ten minutes away. I won't be there more than thirty minutes."

"Who?"

"Who what?"

"Who're you supposed to meet there?"

"It's just a friendly chat. That's all."

"Who? . . . Don't roll your eyes at me. You know it's not safe for you to leave the house. So who is so important that you feel the need to risk your life to go see?"

"It's just . . . it's not what you think. I only need to talk to him for a few minutes."

"Sanders? . . . I knew it. You want to risk your life to go on a date with Sanders? No. Absolutely not."

"It's not a date. God. Why doesn't anybody believe that?"

"Because he's a smarmy little douche who you've already gone on a date with—and kissed. Yeah, I know about the kiss. He told the entire building about it. I wouldn't be surprised if he wrote your names in a heart on a bathroom wall."

"That's ridiculous. And it was one kiss. Not a big deal. And anyway, I regretted it immediately."

"Why?"

"Because I . . . just because. Now, if you'll excuse me, I have to get ready for my *non*-date."

"No."

"I just have to explain to him that I'm not interested. That's it. I don't want to do it on the phone because it's rude not to break bad news to somebody's face. Ugh. Will you move?"

"No."

"Are you jealous? Is that it?"

"Pssh. Please. Jealous of that pip-squeak?"

"You are, aren't you? Your face is twisting itself all up trying to maintain your facade."

"It has nothing to do with Jake or me being jealous. It's the fact that you are mine. Have I not made that clear?"

"Let go of me."

"Do you remember your safe word? . . . Good."

He pushed me back from the doorway, picked me up, and tossed me onto my bed. On my back, leaning on my elbows, I opened my mouth to speak but couldn't. He'd pressed a finger against my lips.

And then he kissed me, not some wimpy love-making kiss, either. It was hungry with lust and ravished my mouth without apology. He made me feel I was the only woman in the world who could satisfy his appetite—and with just a kiss. Then he drew back, pulled my dress up and my panties down. He stared at my wet pussy. "You're so fucking beautiful." In one swipe, he licked my pussy from bottom to top. He resurfaced and kissed me, slipping his fingers inside my pussy. My body quaked. My toes went numb. His fingers moved slowly, yet I imagined the vibrations rippling through me might shatter my body like glass.

"Give me a number."

"Huh?"

"You heard me. Now be a good girl, and give me a number."

"Uh . . . three."

"That a girl. Now I want you to count them out for me. Okay."

"Huh? . . . I don't . . . ohh, I get—"

"Shh."

"Wait—Cooper."

"In Toledo. Now, no more talking."

He lifted my left leg and hooked it around his neck, my heel resting against his spine. Then he ate my pussy with purpose, indelicately, as though there was a prize to be won. His mouth was everywhere at once, lips and clit, above and below, in and out, sucking and biting, flicking and twisting his tongue. I was jittery in a mix of ouch and don't let go. He would caress my thigh at the bend as his shoulder shifted and pressed against it, his wrist bent, his hand occasionally wrapping around to the thigh's inside, a squeeze, and whoa, was I wet. It was so good that I didn't even feel his mouth retreat to speak.

"Was that one?"

"Uh-huhhhhhhh."

"I told you to count 'em out for me." He smacked the side of my ass with a stiff palm.

The sting scattered tingles throughout my body, washing over my skin like an unshakeable shiver. A ringing in my ears.

"Come on. Let me hear you say it."

I unclenched my teeth and took or gave a breath. "One."

"Good girl."

My legs quivered uncontrollably. So many moans. My warm juices cascaded. His tongue rolled around inside me. I reached forward, grabbed his hair, and pushed his head down, thrusting my pussy forward or upward. My clit throbbed for more and none. His hands caressed my hips, gliding to my ribs and slowly sliding back down. Then he grabbed the outside of my legs, near my ass, and bit me. He fucking bit my leg. I screamed in pleasure and fuck all. Goddamnit. Then he slipped his tongue farther inside me than I thought possible. The grip of his hands on my legs was tight and pinched the skin. Everything hurt but didn't. He pulled my pussy against his face, trying to break physical limits. His tongue dragged out and up, darting at and around my clit.

"Twoohoohooh. . . . Are you fucking kidding me?" I attempted to scoot back and quit. No more. I thought I might pass out. "Please . . . I can't . . . Sebast . . . fuck."

"Use your safe word, Laura."

I nodded without a clue of what was rational any more.

"Alright then. You owe me one more. Keep those legs open. That a girl."

I grabbed my breasts. I had to hold on to something. Was he humming? This was insane. And he was still down there. Head bobbing, his intensity became more ferocious each second. I pushed my breasts together. Chewing on my lips, I arched my spine, nearly looking behind me. He snuck a couple fingers inside me and worked my clit with rapturous licks. Or no, he was biting my other leg. But his tongue was in my pussy, bending and curving, flitting about, expanding, extending, diving deeper and deeper, but maybe I was just so numb from the fuck and thunder of it all that I was hallucinating. That's it. I was tripping out. No way any of this was real.

"Threee. . . .

I lay flat, gradually unhanding my breasts. His head rose. He had a glint in his eyes and a glistening smirk. "Good girl. Now I want you to think about this while you're out tonight. And remember that your pussy, your body, every fucking pore of it, belongs to me, for me to do as I please, whenever I want. You are mine. Understand? . . . Good girl."

16

Sebastian

"Where the fuck have you been? We agreed. You said you'd be back in less than an hour. It's been almost two. What the fuck, Laura? I thought something had happened to you. I knew this was a bad idea. I don't know why I caved."

"I'm sorry. He didn't take the news well. He seemed to think we were an item or something. I couldn't just leave him there weeping over a steak. Anyway, I'm here, and I'm fine. You can stop worrying."

"No, I won't stop worrying. I can't, not until this thing is over. Shit, Laura, I'd started making calls to assemble a team to look for you. I thought you'd been abducted."

"Well, look no further. I'm here."

"That's it." I grabbed her wrist and pulled her toward the couches. "If you can't treat me with respect and drop the sassy brat routine, then I'll just have to punish you."

"Ooohhh."

"Why must you toy with me? Do you like when I punish you? Is that it? Fine by me. You know the drill. Get on my lap."

She pulled up her dress, smirked, and lay across my legs. The way her panties cradled her ass, accentuating the cheeks and their curves, was sexy and alluring. I rubbed a bare spot of cheek and gave it a few pats and then—smack. "Is this what you want?"

She moaned with a hum.

"I think you owe me—(slap)—a proper apology."

"I'm sorry for—"

Slap. "Look up at me when you speak."

"I'm . . ." she swallowed, her eyes moistening. "I'm sorry."

Slap. "Sorry for what?"

Whether it was an act or not, I don't know, but when she looked at me, she had half a grin. It was subtle and nearly overshadowed by the teardrop falling to the floor. Yet I recognized it.

"I'm sorry for being late and . . . and not taking you seriously."

"Good girl." Slap. "Now prove to me how sorry you really are. Ride my cock."

She stood, removed her dress over the shoulders, and tossed it aside.

"Good girl."

She smiled.

"Now drop those panties."

I rose from the couch, lowered my pants and briefs, and sat back down. She climbed aboard, grabbed my cock, and guided it in as she sank, submerging my cock in what felt like a million different wet sensations. Nothing had ever felt so warm and right, the perfect fit.

"Is this what you wanted?" Moaning, she swayed her hips, gliding up and down. "Fuhhck. It goes so deep."

"That a girl." I rubbed her clit, circles and x's, and figure eights. She moaned within her moans. Her head fell back. Her pussy tightened around my cock, the muscles contracting. Shit, not yet. I wasn't done with her.

"Okay, on your knees. I want to finish off in your mouth."

I'd never seen my cock this large. Throbbing, it felt twice its size. It stared at the ceiling, shimmering wet. Maybe it was an illusion.

She adjusted her knees, gave my cock a few warm-up strokes, then opened wide and wrapped her lips around it. I grabbed the hair around the back of her head, pushed and shoved, jamming my cock in her mouth. She gagged, tried to pull back, felt the resistance from my hand blocking her head, and stayed put. I gave her a second, then swung my hips. Her teeth grazed my shaft. I thought her eyes might pop. She peered up at me, proud of herself, tears wrecking her mascara. That sight never got old. A few more thrusts and come burst from my cock, throbbing harder with each spurt. I released her hair. She gagged while swallowing and trying to breathe.

She wiped a corner of her mouth with the back of her hand, then grinned devilishly.

"Good girl."

17

Laura

Lilac. That's all I had to say. But I didn't because I was right where I wanted to be. So spare me your judgments. Don't mistake my tears for sorrow, my gagging for choking, or my submissiveness for weakness. I knew what I was doing. And I relished every sting and ache, every sticky drip, and I craved more.

Love. Well, I can't say I wasn't pondering the word, especially since I was bored in that big house, lazing about, nurturing my thoughts. I guess you can say I was in that weird gray area, wondering if he liked me as much as I liked him. All I knew was my feelings for Sebastian were stronger than I'd ever had for any man. It was one of those moments when you question whether you've ever really been in love, despite having previously said those three words to others. You know what I mean?

Cooper had returned but had been in his home office all day. Sebastian was busy plotting how to save my life and bring down a global trafficking organization. So I was surprised when he texted me and said we were going to dinner.

He said to wear the black dress I'd worn in Colombia, which reminded me of Colombia and the pool and my first spanking and his cock and—phew. I had to sit for a bit, take a breath, and fight the urge to masturbate, a weird sensation because I'd never really been much of a masturbator. I always felt so alone afterward. Yet now was not the time for reflecting on masturbatory emotions. I still needed to get dressed, do my makeup, and style my hair.

Sebastian stood at the bottom step, his hands clasped in front of him. I was getting good at slowly strutting down the stairs in pretty dresses while his eyes smothered me in his awe between blinks.

"Look at you. Absolutely gorgeous. Stunning is more like it."

"Thank you. Then again, you could say anything when wearing a black suit and knock me off my feet. So handsome."

"Shall we?"

"You haven't told me where we're going yet."

"It's a surprise."

It was a formal restaurant, posh and dazzling. Dim lighting. The sound of a violin whispering over unseen speakers. Elegant dark wood. A gray marble counter at the bar. We had a private booth. A view of a lake. The moon hung low, hooking into the horizon, splashing white light over the lake's face. Stars dappled the sky.

The waiter brought a bottle of Dom Perignon, poured a dab in each glass, then wriggled the bottle into the ice bucket on the table's middle. Sebastian ordered for me, speaking in what was obviously choppy Italian, weaving English in whenever he couldn't muster the right word. His stuttering was cute.

A man wearing a tuxedo with a black bowtie stopped by the table immediately after the waiter had scurried off. He and Sebastian were on a first-name basis. Dante folded over, his hands behind his back, and whispered in Sebastian's ear. Sebastian chuckled. I pretended not to be upset. Dante stood straight, said it was nice seeing him, that it had been a long time, too long, have to meet up soon, hit the links. Then he left.

"Who was that?"

"I met him on a business trip. A long time ago. He owns the place."

"Ohh. He seems nice. It's a beautiful restaurant."

"Yeah, he's done well for himself. Listen, the reason I asked you here—"

"Oh, God. Is this the part where you tell me we have to stop having sex and pretend like nothing ever happened? Let me guess: I'm too young. You can't be with your best friend's sister. Let's just be friends—blah blah blah."

"What? No, it's nothing like that. However, on a sidenote, I think Cooper might know because this morning he found a pair of your underwear in the living room, the pair you were wearing last night."

"Ohhh. . . ."

"Yeah. He asked if you'd had any guys over. I said I didn't know. Then he asked if you were still dating Jake. I said I thought you were. . . . Sorry. I had to think fast, and it seemed the right move at the time. I wasn't prepared to defend myself or give a confession."

The waiter brought our food. Sebastian's steak looked as though it might moo. I plucked off the hard-boiled eggs from my salad I'd asked the waiter to exclude. Yellow crumbles remained between the romaine leaves. Sebastian effortlessly cut into his steak. I glared at my salad.

"So wait, why do you think Cooper believes we are, you know, involved? It seems like you covered your tracks well enough. And my underwear could've wound up in the living room any number of ways."

"Right, I got ahead of myself. Before he'd stood in my doorway holding a pencil with your underwear hanging off the end of it, we were in the gym shooting the shit after a workout, and he asked what we were doing the morning we had our hands in the sink, you know, before he walked in. We shared a guilty look, he said. I said we'd had a rough start to our working relationship and so I'd made us breakfast to bury the hatchet and start fresh. He said that didn't sound like me at all. I agreed but said I was turning over a new leaf. He asked who the girl was. Because, in his eyes, only a woman could possibly turn me soft, which was still unlikely, he said. There is no woman, I said. Then I made up some bullshit about how things had been going really well for me at work and with the case and this, that, and the other thing. Anyway, back to the underwear—at first, he thought your lacey piece was evidence that I was seeing somebody and had fucked her in the living room. After I said no, no women had been to the house, it only left you as the possible owner of the underpants. Are you laughing?"

"Underpants?"

"I don't know why I said that. Go on, let it out. I'll wait here. . . . Are you good? . . . Honestly, I thought you'd take this more seriously."

"No, I am. It's just . . . sometimes when I'm nervous, I laugh, and this night, you, everything that's happening, has happened, it's all too much. I don't know whether to laugh, cry, or hide. And Cooper, he's the least of my worries. Come on, tell me whatever it is you brought me here to tell me. I'm ready."

"You're really something, you know that?"

"You're stalling again, not that I don't want to hear more. I do. But let's rip off the Band Aid and get on with it."

"You're not going to like it. I don't like it. But our options are limited. Before I even begin, I want you to know you are under no obligation to do this. If you say no, I'll drop it. You won't hear another word about it from me."

"Stalling."

"Okay, well . . . is there something wrong with your salad? . . . Alright, alright. So, I talked to my friend, Matt, this morning, after the underwear incident. Matt's the one who's been helping me with the trafficking case. And he's concocted a plan to potentially nail these guys—but it's risky . . . and it involves you. . . ."

"I'm listening."

"So, we have the company's anniversary party this weekend and—"

"But that'll be too late, won't it? That's the day after the deadline. That man said—"

"It has to be that day. Let me finish, and you'll understand why. So, you and I will attend the party together. It's at Anderson Tech, per usual, and, as you know, there's no corner of that building where a camera doesn't point. But here's where the risky part comes in, the part that involves you. We need you to wander off, away from the party, and use the first restroom on the second floor, the one right outside the elevators. . . . That's the point. Because they still won't have the drive, the traffickers will probably send that man to the party, and he'll be watching you, waiting for an opportunity to get you alone."

"You wanna use me as bait? You're joking, right?"

"How's your steak, sir? Excellent. And is it cooked to your liking? Good to hear. And you, madam? . . . Are you sure? You've barely touched it. . . . I understand. Would we like another bottle of Dom Perignon? Very well then. Enjoy."

"Listen, Laura, there will be undercover cops inside the building and patrol cars outside, parked a few blocks away. And I'll have members of my team there making sure everything runs smoothly and that no harm comes to you. Not to mention, I'll be by your side all night—except for, you know, when you step away."

"I don't like it. No way. It's too dangerous. What's to stop him from shooting me in there?"

"No, no, he won't shoot you. That'd be too loud. And it's highly unlikely he would kill you at Anderson Tech—too many witnesses, too many people who'll see his face. And these guys are pros. They won't leave a body behind, and there's no way anybody would be able to remove a dead body or even abduct a live one from that party without a hundred people seeing it. And with all the police and my team and the cameras, we'll have this guy cornered."

"Okay. So suppose for some wildly insane reason I agree to do this, provided the plan works, and you catch the guy, then what? How'll that make a lick of difference? He's just one guy."

"Well, you're right. He is only one man. And catching him is just half the plan. The other half involves interrogating him, prying information from him. And if we're lucky, if the police don't fuck it all up, we can get this guy to flip on his crew. Then we nail his crew and repeat the process, though hopefully we get enough from this asshole to end it for good, or at least gather enough evidence from taking down his crew to put the entire organization away."

"It seems like a lot of things need to go right in order for this plan to work. What about Cooper? How does he feel about this?"

"Ehh . . . he doesn't know about it. Not yet. I wanted to run it by you first. I saw no point in getting him riled up without knowing whether you would even do it. And let's be clear about one thing, when Matt presented this to me, my answer was a hard no. I still don't like the idea of using you as bait. It's unnerving, just the though of it. But we have nothing else. When I said our options were limited, I meant this is our only option. However, you say the word, and we don't do it. That I even brought this to you makes me question my judgment. If anything were to happen to you, I would never, ever, be able to live with myself. I promise, if you agree to do this, not that I'm trying to sell it to you, but if you agree to it, I will do everything in my power to ensure you leave that party unharmed and with me."

"I have to think about it."

"I hate to pressure you, Laura, but you'll have to decide by the end of the night. We only have four days till the party. And we have a lot of work to do to prepare if you decide to go through with it."

"And then there's Cooper."

"And then there's Cooper."

"I have to use the restroom."

"Are you alright?"

"Yeah, I just have to pee."

"Okay. If the waiter comes by, do you want me to have him box up your salad?"

"Sure."

I was mad but not at him, mostly at the situation and, of course, the degenerate pricks responsible for this mess. Then again, couldn't Sebastian be partly or wholly to blame? If he hadn't stolen their files, I wouldn't be pondering using myself as bait, putting myself in a possibly deadly position.

Yet I couldn't be mad at him. He was, after all, trying to save me, despite having ulterior motives.

The women's room smelled of citrus, was tiny with three stalls, and the partitions were made of finished wood, darker than cherry. The mirrors had gilded, Victorian-esque frames. The sinks were large ceramic bowls. The lighting matched the dining area, low and comforting.

The enchantment of the bathroom soothed me. But then, as I was peeing, somebody with a deep voice mumbled in the stall next. I was certain it was a man. He sounded drunk and mad. He banged on the partition. I lifted my feet and tucked my knees under my chin, my underwear around my ankles. He banged again. "Hand me some toilet paper. I'm all out." Had I gone into the wrong bathroom? No, I was sure I'd read the sign correctly and saw the triangular skirt on the little figure.

"Hey. I know you're in there. Gimme some goddamn toilet paper." Banging, "For cryin' out loud, lady. Don't make me come in there." His hand waved below the partition. He had a barcode tattooed on it. Could it be? It didn't sound like the gunman from my car at all. What if he was acting, putting on a show in hopes of catching me off guard? But I still had four days. Maybe he was trying to send me a message to let me know he was watching me. Shit.

"Sweetheart, I don't have all night."

I would never use a public bathroom again. That was the promise I made to myself, his hand flapping around, all hairy with fat knuckles and that tattoo. Then he pounded on the partition again. "Quit being a bitch and help me out."

I closed my eyes—because that is how you become invisible. I felt the toilet rattle each time he hit the partition. I might've imagined it. A screeching rang in my ears. I opened my eyes. He pulled up his black slacks, his belt clanking. The screeching was in my head. I knew it but couldn't fight it off. He neared his door. "I'm coming for you." I quickly yanked up my underwear and unlocked the door. One. Two. Three. "Hey sweetheart. You're better lookin' than I imagined." It wasn't the gunman.

His breath smelled of onions and gin. He was unshaven. His tie was loosened, and he had what might've been a hickey on his neck. My heart raced. I thought I might faint. My hands trembled. Then a fist smashed into his jaw. He went limp and dropped to the tiled floor. A thud.

Sebastian stepped into my view, standing before the stall's doorway. His face, solemn and kind, exuded safety, while his sky-blue eyes told me a love story. "Come on, let's get you home." He took my hand and my heart.

18
Laura

"I'll do it."

"You'll do what?"

"The plan, using me as bait, I want to do it."

"Are you sure? Maybe it'd be best to wait till we're home and you've calmed down a bit. You just had a big scare back there. You're not thinking clearly."

"I've never thought so clearly in my life. I won't change my mind. I'm tired of living in fear."

"I don't know, Laura. I was having difficulty accepting this plan in general. And now that you've agreed to do it, I just . . . maybe there's another way, one that doesn't involve putting your life at risk."

"There's not, you said so yourself. This is our only option. So I'm doing it."

"And Cooper?"

"He's my brother, not my owner. He'll just have to deal with it. He can get on board, help keep me safe, or he can get out of the way. It's time he realizes I'm his sibling, his equal, not his kid sister."

"Listen to you. How can I even argue with you right now?"

"Hey, this isn't the way home? Where're we going?"

"I have an idea, something to cheer you up."

"Ohh. . . ."

"That boutique you like, the one with the dresses you're always window shopping, do you think it's open this late?"

"It's only 7:30. They must be. Wait, why?"

"Well, you'll need a dress for the party, won't you?"

It took me only three seconds to find the dress I wanted, strapless in red. It looked as sleek on me as it had on the mannequin last week when I'd gawked at it from the sidewalk, daydreaming.

"Hey, can you come help me? The zipper is stuck."

"I'm going to pretend like I haven't heard that one before."

It's such a cliche, I know. But I'd never done it before. The anticipation alone was exhilarating. I cracked the door. He stood there, hands in his pockets, rocking on his heels, fake whistling. "I'm here about the zipper."

"Shh, quick, get in. . . . 'I'm here about the zipper,' really? What are you, auditioning for a porno?"

"And how would you know?"

"Never mind that. Here, I can't reach it." I held up my hair with one hand, the dress by the chest with the other. I watched him over my shoulder, imagining what he saw, what his view was. The way my arm beside my head formed a partial triangle. Short strands of honey-colored hair lingering about my slender neck. The birthmark on my left shoulder that I'm self-conscious about. My gooseflesh. I pictured the dimple above my ass, just before the spine curves and the knobs show. Then he reached for the zipper. And I let go of the dress.

"Wow. . . . How? How is it even possible that such a flawless creature exists? You are remarkable."

"Are you done talking?"

"Turn around."

Behind him was a mirror. Looking over his shoulder, I'd never seen my face look so happy, so flush from affection and lust, or was it a yearning now, no, a longing, a seemingly undying urge for more and all of him all at once.

He went behind me, his eyes not letting go of my body. "You're going to watch me play with you. Do not make a sound. Understand? . . . Good girl."

His palms grazed my shoulders, traveled lightly down my arms, then upward over my hips, the backs of his hands brushing against the inside of my arms. My nipples hardened. His palms touched my ribs, skimming to the front. A shiver. He cupped my breasts and briefly massaged them, followed by a gentle squeeze and release. A tingle tickled me everywhere. Back down, his hands glided over my stomach. I gasped as he pressed the creases between my thighs and pussy, dragging his hands upward, pressing. I was entranced.

He grabbed and pushed up my chin. "Watch the mirror, not my hands. I don't want you to miss a thing."

Down went my panties. His breath blew warm but calm against my ass. I stepped out of the lacey leg holes and toe-flicked them aside. He repositioned my head, setting it forward, chin level, a finger on my lips. "Eyes straight ahead. Watch. . . . Good girl."

His index finger tugged my bottom lip when he dropped his hand, his fingers curled, swiping between my breasts, then my stomach, still grazing, then my clit. He pulled his middle finger upward through my southern lips, a fingertip peeking inside my pussy. I had difficulty standing still. My quivering wrecked my balance. He licked my neck, stretched my earlobe with his teeth, then whispered, "Shh," as he slipped a few fingers inside me. I cupped a hand over my mouth, catching a gasp, and nearly rolled my left ankle.

"Quiet." His chin on my shoulder, he fingered my pussy at various speeds, slow for three strokes, fast for four, clit rub, working the thumb, multi-tasking. At the bend where my neck meets my shoulder, he bit me. I shivered and jerked.

He unzipped his pants, then pushed me toward the wall. "Put your hands up on the mirror. Spread your legs. Stay still and silent."

He shoved his cock into me. Its throb pulsed throughout my body. I swallowed a scream, gnawing on my tongue. He thrust his cock in deeper. I stifled a squeal. He pinned my hands against the mirror, bent his knees a bit, then thrust upward. A pause. Warm juices dribbled down my legs. He leaned into my ass, trying to put his cock in farther, and gyrated a little, rolling his cock around in my pussy while intermittently leaning into it. My head toppled backward. And I moaned.

"Do I need to stop?"

"No, I'm sorry—I'll be quiet. I promise. Please, whatever you do, do not stop."

He covered my mouth, pinching my cheeks, and wrapped an arm around my waist. He fucked me fast and hard, slamming into me, pelvis to ass, cock in pussy. I bit one of his fingers. He shoved me against the mirror. My breasts flattened, and my face turned sideways, squishing my reflection. He pumped away with no rhythm, just crashing into me. The mirror muffled my moans. Both hands holding my hips, he pulled me into him, thrusting powerfully. My legs twitched, weakening. I couldn't hold myself up much longer. I groaned, full of so much come. His panting breezed warmly against my ear. My hair scraped my back. I licked my lips, imagining I could taste his come. My eyes danced, the orgasm wavering. Thank fucking Christ.

He slid his cock out. I jumped, gasping. My knees buckled when my weight came down on them. He swung an arm around my waist and pulled me up, his fat cock slippery against my ass, his come sticking to my dimple. I glanced over my shoulder, my hands on the mirror. "You . . . I love the way you—the way you fuck me. It's . . . incredible."

The dress lay boxed on my lap. I ran a finger over the box's textured gold letters. "Can't it wait till morning?"

"No, we have to tell him tonight. Besides, the man is a bear in the morning."

"Am I telling him, or are you?"

"We tell him together."

"I like the sound of that, together."

"Yeah, maybe hide that face when we talk to Cooper."

"What face? It's the only one I have."

"You know what I mean. . . . No, no, you stay put. I'll get the door. Your hands are full."

"What a sweetheart."

"Don't tell anyone."

"Thank you. . . . How do I look?"

"Like you just . . . maybe pat your hair down or something."

I crouched, pushed in the side-view mirror, and adjusted its angle. "Hold on. I think I have a hairtie in my purse. . . . Better?"

"Much. Ready?"

"Ready as I'll ever be."

"Have you lost your fuckin' mind? As if you fucking my sister weren't bad enough—yeah, I know your fucking. The last three times I've seen her, she's had that creepy glow, like the one she's wearing now—that freshly fucked face. And you, you fucking asshole, suddenly you're nice to her, doing the dishes together. How stupid do you think I am? And now you wanna use her as bait in your little scheme to take down a global crime syndicate whose primary source of income is trafficking young women for sex. Do you know what they do to those girls? They get them hooked on heroin, keep 'em drugged and fucked stupid until they're nothing but doped-out rag dolls. Is that what you want to be, Laura, a smack addict whose sole purpose is to get fucked by the highest bidder? When did you get so brazenly stupid? It's him, isn't it? What manipulative bullshit has this womanizing asshole done to make you think throwing yourself at a hitman is a jolly fucking good time on a Saturday night? Tell me, one of you, why the fuck any of this is happening?"

"Okay, Coop, you need to calm down. Jesus. First off, I fuck who I want, how I want, when I want, wherever the fuck I want. I'm my own person. I make my decisions, not you. And if I want to put my life at risk to save not only my life but yours, too, yes, your life is on the line here too—and think of all the girls held captive right this minute, and the ones who'll be abducted tonight, tomorrow, next week, and on and on. Honestly, the more I think of it, the more I want to go through with it. I could save thousands of lives. So why the fuck wouldn't I use myself as bait, huh? It would be selfish and negligent for me to walk away knowing I could help."

"Listen, Cooper—"

"Shut up. Nobody's talking to you right now. This is a family matter."

"Bullshit. I am family and you know it. You and I go way back. Now I know you're pissed off, and I would be too. I get it. But the plan is solid. Nothing's going to happen to her. I promise. I already told you of the manpower we'll have there, and I want you there too, to make sure everything runs smoothly. You've always had a knack for seeing the little things and predicting when shit's about to go wrong. I need, no, we need you to set aside your anger and work with us, not against us. I'm even willing to look past all the bad shit you just said about me to make this work."

"Fuck you."

"Coop. Stop blaming Sebastian. You're mad. And that's understandable, but—"

"I'm mad. Your both fucking nuts. And if he'd never taken their files, none of this would ever have happened, and we wouldn't be standing here contemplating handing you over to sexual predators. The way I see it, this is all his fault. The only way you could possibly see it any differently would be if you were fucking him. Oh, that's right—you are! On what planet . . . no, you know what? I have nothing else to say here. Laura, I wish you the best, and I hope nothing happens to you, but I can't take part in it. I just . . . I can't. I'm outta here."

"Coop! Where're you going?"

"Just let him go. He'll cool off."

"Do you really believe that, or are you just trying to comfort me?"

"Both."

"Now what?"

19

Laura

"Can we take a break? I feel like I might pass out."

"Only because you did so well on the last run through. Just remember, keep your stance wide so your balance stays centered and no matter what you do, do not hesitate. Many great men have lost their lives from hesitating. And don't forget to really snap that kick out, using your back leg, then run."

"Do you really think I'll need to know any of this stuff?"

"Let's hope not. But I thought it would be best to teach you a few techniques just in case. It doesn't hurt to be prepared. However, I don't think you will be put in a position where you need to defend yourself. Matt and I will be in the men's room next door, and today we're installing an additional camera, hidden, aimed directly at the women's room door. The second we see anybody go in the bathroom, Matt and I will rush in and grab him."

"Have you heard from Cooper?"

"No, but it hasn't even been twelve hours. He's probably sleeping off a long night, likely passed out on the couch in his office. He'll come around."

"I hope so. Ugh, I'm so sweaty. Are we done? I need a hot shower. Wanna join me?"

"I have a better idea."

"Oh really." He picked me up, holding me sideways by the legs and back. "Are you going to carry me all the way to the bathroom?"

"You'll see."

He threw me onto his bed. I bounced and giggled and nearly rolled onto the floor. "Hey, are these what I think they are?"

"You're about to find out. And . . . I have a surprise for you, which I'm certain you'll enjoy. Now—take off your clothes, except for the panties. Leave those on, then lay on your back on the middle of the bed."

Below the mattress's sides, black straps hung from the bed frame, two on either side. Leather cuffs were attached to the end of the straps. As he restrained my right ankle, tucking the strap's end through its buckle, butterflies wreaked havoc in my stomach. Yet I was giddy. Once my wrists and ankles were secured, he pulled from under the bed a short metal bar thinner than a broomstick. It had what looked like keyrings connected to its ends. He placed the bar between my ankles and, with carabiners, clipped each end onto a metal ring sticking out of the restraints.

"What are you going to do me?"

"That's so you can't close your legs."

"Yeah, but what are you planning to do to me?"

"What's your safe word?"

"Lilac."

"Good girl."

"You still didn't answer me."

"You'll see."

He went to the closet and, from its top shelf, grabbed a black box with metal trim along its edges and corners, big enough to fit three pairs of my shoes. He set it on the dresser. He snapped its latch open and removed a small pink object that almost looked like a vibrator but bigger and unlike any I'd ever seen. It had a rubber extension, short and circular, its middle hollow.

Sitting on the bed's edge, he slipped the pink thing beneath my panties. The rubber piece circled my clit. He pushed a button.

Holy fucking hell.

Whatever this contraption was, while vibrating, it sucked on my clit with quick bursts of suction.

I jolted. My thighs rumbled. "Sebastian . . . what the. . . ."

He pushed the button again, increasing the object's intensity. Then he adjusted my panties to hold that pink monster in place.

"I thought you might like that. I'll leave the bathroom door open, so I can hear you shout in case it becomes too much and you need to use your safe word.

"Whh-ha-ha-hat? Sebast . . . but I . . . I'm about to. . . ."

He turned the corner, and I orgasmed. Yes, already. Picture me lying there on the bed, my limbs stretched out and cuffed. I couldn't close my legs, scratch an itch, or move that pink devil an inch. I tried to wiggle my hips and knock that sucker loose but to no avail. My legs were spasming. I was sweating. Even my cheeks trembled.

Another orgasm quivered closer. Every muscle in my body tightened. I arched my back as best I could and looked at the headboard. My eyes flipped back, tweaking, reaching for an understanding. I thought I might die of pleasure, just convulse from so many orgasms and croak in a lake of my juices. To say I moaned would be an understatement. I fucking howled.

Orgasm number three approached with such insanity that my jaw locked. My teeth clenched. The room twirled. I felt as though I were spiraling. The ceiling seemed to get farther and farther away. I shook my hips, yanked on the restraints, and rocked my head. I was practically drooling. I couldn't say no, let alone lilac, not that I wanted the ride to stop. I didn't. Yet I might've turned that little beast off had my limbs not been shackled and numb. I'm kidding. No fucking way. To say it was incredible would be an understatement. I felt as if I'd been blessed with the mouth of an erotic angel with a grudge. I had arrived.

"Laura. Are you okay?"

I grunted or moaned. Maybe I shook my head. Likely I was noiseless and motionless. I don't know. My body was there, but I was elsewhere.

He undid the restraints, kissing my forehead while setting my hands free. "You're such a good girl." He removed the bar holding my legs apart. My feet flopped inward. He unbuckled my ankles. If I had the energy or the wherewithal, I could've done jumping jacks or walked.

Wearing only a towel, he lay on his side beside me, resting his head on a palm, wet hair, an elbow digging into the comforter. I nestled my nose against his chest, moaning weakly. Just a purr. Still swirling in an orgasm-induced dream caused by a clitoral vacuum, trying to control the tremulous aftershock, I rolled my head, peered up at his chin, and said, "That was fucking insane."

"I'm not done yet. Are you up for another surprise?"

"Mmhm."

"That a girl. I think you may like this, too. But you won't be able to use your safe word, so if you want me to stop, just squeeze my wrist. Understand?"

I nodded with a yes that barely squeaked out.

Is it crazy how much I trusted this man? I mean—there was nothing I wouldn't let him do to me. And now my old life seemed like medieval times, the dark ages, clumsy and soft, uneventful. I couldn't return to missionary sex with the lights off, awkward thrusts, sympathetic cuddling, and over-apologetic men who ask to kiss before kissing. Fuck that.

A world without Sebastian was a world I did not want to fuck in.

He turned away and swung his feet off the bed, stood, and whipped off the towel around his waist. His cock was hard, just for me. He propped my legs on his shoulders, the crooks of my knees resting on his clavicles. Then his massive cock slid into my dripping wet pussy.

"Fuck, Laura. I'ts like your pussy was the mold that shaped my cock. Could you be any more perfect?"

Was I supposed to answer that? Nah-uh. Why ruin such a fantastic compliment by speaking. I smiled, then bit my bottom lip with a half-nod.

His thrusts quickly turned vigorous. My ass cheeks jiggled, my head tapping the headboard. Back and forth, my body jerked as he pounded into me. Then his hand was on my throat, applying pressure. I couldn't breathe. I touched his wrist but didn't squeeze it. I tried to gasp but hardly rasped. His thrusts had slowed and had twice the impact. Swing back, slam. My eyelids tried to shut, would flutter, close for a touch, open for a wink, then repeat. As he slowly released the pressure on my throat, he increased the speed of his thrusts from slow and slamming to pounding jabs. The second air hit my lungs, hot liquid sprayed Sebastian's chest and splashed onto me. He didn't budge, just kept fucking me as though nothing had happened.

"Baby . . . you just . . . squirted . . . all . . . over . . . me." His cock went off like a jet stream inside me. His hips slowed. Then he relaxed, panting, and sat there, letting his dick go limp in my pussy while my legs twitched on his shoulders.

"That's never happened to me before. I'm embarrassed. I'm so sorry."

"Why are you sorry? I fucking loved it."

20

Sebastian

Then Murray slit my throat with a seven-inch blade. Blood oozed down my dream's image as I'd seen in horror flicks when it seemed the inside of the television's screen was covered in blood. I awakened, more frightened than usual. The nightmares had become less frequent yet more intense. This was only my second one since returning from Colombia.

I'd left the bedside lamp on, was still in my clothes, and sweating from head to toe. I dropped my pants and briefs, sat on the bed's edge, and grabbed the box cutter from between the mattresses. I peeled off the bandage on my inner thigh and lost a few hairs. It stung. I didn't need the bandage. It covered the scars surrounding the scab of my last cut, preventing Laura from asking further questions. That she hadn't inquired more about what was beneath the bandage was surprising. The power of sex, I suppose.

I pushed the box cutter's blade up, took and held a breath, then pressed the blade's tip against the skin hard enough to indent the flesh but not break it. I thought about it. This was usually an unthinking process, a nearly automatic response whose purpose was self-punishment and distraction. But I thought about it. Why?

Too deep a question for the middle of the night.

I put the box cutter away, then ran a hand over my brow. My phone buzzed beside the lamp's base.

"Yeah."

"You sound like shit."

"It's the middle of the night, Matt. Get to the point."

"What're you drunk? It's six p.m. You need to meet me at Anderson Tech in an hour. The officers are already in place. And we've got three UCs disguised as waiters and two as guests. Everything's in order."

"Of course I'm not fucking drunk. I must've dozed off after my workout. Your call woke me up. Nothing to worry about. Did you go in this morning and double-check all the cameras are working? . . . And the new one? . . . Good. I'll see you in an hour. Oh, and Matt . . . thank you."

I lurked in Laura's doorway, watching her stand before a full-length mirror, struggling to poke an earring through her left ear, her neck bent. The red dress we'd bought her advertised her hips so well that she looked as though she were wearing a corset.

"Do you need some help?"

"Ooh, you scared me. How long have you been standing there?"

"Long enough to imagine that dress on the floor."

Her mirrored smile warmed my heart. Wait, what? That's not right. Ahem—her mirrored smile woke my cock. Forget it.

She spun around, then ran her palms from her hips to her thighs and put one foot forward. "What do you think?"

"I think you belong on a runway. You're ravishing. Stunning. Beautiful. Absolutely fucking gorgeous. And I think I'll have trouble keeping my hands off you tonight."

"Just tonight?"

"Oh no, this is a daily struggle."

"Well, you look really handsome, even in those sweaty gym clothes. You need to get ready."

I walked over to her. "I will. But first I need to ensure this dress fits you properly." I reached around her, rubbed her ass cheeks, squeezed, then pulled her against me, shoving her pussy at my cock.

"Mmhm. There's something about your hands. They just feel so . . . magical. And as badly as I want them all over me right now, we need to focus. Go get dressed."

"I'm worried."

"You should be. So am I. But what choice do we have?"

"Maybe we don't have to do it. Maybe there's another way. I'll find one. There must be a different option. There has to be, right?"

"I'm not backing out, Sebastian. And you know this is our only option. I've got this."

"You're right. Last minute jitters, I guess." I kissed her, caressing her ass. "This dress is getting me all worked up."

"Well, work yourself down. We don't have time for sex."

"Nonsense." I flipped the front of her dress up and pulled it over her head, blindfolding her. She squealed. I yanked down her panties, red lace. "Lift your left foot . . . now the right. Good girl. Now, the way I see it is we have at least thirty minutes before we must leave, which leaves me plenty of time to play with you. What do you think?"

"I'm ready."

"Can you breathe alright under there?"

"Uh-huh."

"And you know your safe word."

"Lilac."

"Good girl."

I spread her lips and licked upward through the middle, wetting my nose. Between her legs, I reached behind her and lightly dragged a finger down her ass's middle. She squirmed, either tickled or afraid. Her giggle was misleading. I sucked on her clit, intermittently batting it with my tongue's tip without removing my lips, quick flicks. Then I moved three fingers inside her while working my mouth on her pulsating clit. Her moan touched my tongue. I grabbed her thighs and licked my way north, dragging my tongue around and over her navel. I bit one bra-covered breast, tugging on her nipple. Then I kissed her fabric-covered lips, pulling down on the dress behind her head, sliding two fingers into her pussy, stroking gently while my thumb fiddled with her clit. The moan she hummed through the fabric vibrated in my mouth.

I whispered in her ear. "I want you to ride my cock again. Take my hand." I walked her over to the desk near the doorway. I dropped my sweats and briefs. I spun the chair at the desk around and pulled it away from the desk. I turned her back to me, and I sat down. My cock stood tall and throbbed. I grabbed her hand and placed it on my cock. "I'm right here."

"Jesus, Sebastian. It feels even bigger when I can't see it. It has a heartbeat."

I guided her backward by her hips. As she nervously lowered her ass, I aimed my cock, and told her to drop down. The chair swiveled. I held her breasts so she wouldn't fall over. "Now ride."

She had some energy in her tonight. She bounced on my cock. She was fast and enthusiastic. The chair wouldn't stay still. She hopped, her weight crashing down on me. Once, she raised herself too high, and my cock came completely out, and when she dropped back down, she almost snapped my dick in half.

When I spoke, it sounded as if I were speaking into a fan. "Wh-at-'s got-ten in-to yo-u?"

She didn't say anything because I had my hand on her throat. Did I forget to mention that? Not too hard, just enough pressure to make it interesting. I gave her a little squeeze, then let up, and so on. My left hand moved to her clit, though I had difficulty keeping my hand steady with her hopping. I managed.

The chair had rolled back against the desk. A lamp fell. I put pressure on her throat, my fingers rubbing her clit any which way. The desk smashed against the wall each time she landed on my cock. A painting fell, hit the desk, collapsed, and touched my back. I was half a stroke from coming, and she showed no signs of slowing down.

I pinched her throat. "Remember, if you want me to stop, squeeze my wrist."

"Mmhm."

The dress slid down her face from my hand on her neck. Her bouncing slowed to a casual ride, then she leaned forward a tick and worked her hips, rocking and grinding. I stretched the dress back over her head, pulling her backward and tearing the fabric. I grabbed her throat, still holding the dress taut. I squeezed her throat for ten seconds, then simultaneously let go of her throat and the dress. She screamed ecstatically and fell forward onto the floor. My come squirted, arched, and landed on her backside, sticking to her dress.

"Holy shit. Laura, are you okay?"

She chuckled, deep breaths, her palms on the floor, head downturned. "That was fantastic."

"I think you need a new dress."

"What? Why?"

"Uhh . . . it's a little sticky now. And I'm pretty sure I ripped the front of it."

She rolled over, sat, and looked at the dress's front. "Damnit. I love this dress."

"Yeah, but you wear that black one just as well. It doesn't matter. You could go in a trash bag with holes cut out for the limbs and your head and you'd still be the most beautiful girl in the room."

"You're only saying that because your dick was just inside me."

"Come here."

She picked herself up, pulled the dress over her shoulders, and threw it on the desk behind me. Her bra was crooked, one breast trying to escape. The lamp on the floor shone perfectly on her wet thighs, and her pussy twinkled. She went to sit on my lap but stopped and stood straight. "What is that?"

"What?"

"You said in Colombia that you'd had a drunken accident. Remember, you had a bandage on your leg? But what are all those scars?"

"All you need to know is that those are from a previous life, one I'd rather not talk about right now. That's not who I am anymore. Besides, we don't have the time."

"Well, it's just...."

"What is it?"

She sat on my lap, bringing my cock back to life. I tossed an arm around her and rubbed her thigh.

"It's just . . . I'm already confused about what's going on with us. And when you shut me out like that, I get even more confused."

"What do you mean?"

"I know we've only had sex a handful of times, but still, a girl's gotta ask, you know?"

"I don't follow."

"What are we doing? Am I just another fuck to you, or is this something more?"

"That's a pretty heavy question for two people who are about to undertake a covert operation with their lives at stake. Don't you think?"

"When you put it like that, I feel stupid and selfish. Thanks."

Did I love her? Did I want more than sex, more than another sub who'd bend to my will and fulfill my every whim? I hadn't given it much thought.

Until now.

21

Laura

I was more mad at not knowing our status than at him. I left the room out of frustration, not anger. But I pushed aside our personal matters and smiled as we walked arm-and-arm into Anderson Tech.

The party was held in the lobby, a room with two balconies and a waterfall gliding down the far wall between two staircases facing one another. We weren't five feet passed the entrance when somebody shouted for Sebastian. He turned around. "Lucas. Holy shit. How long's it been?"

Lucas gave Sebastian a hug, then patted his shoulder. "Too long, my friend, too long. And who's this beauty?"

"This is my friend Laura. Laura, this is Lucas. We were in the Navy together, three tours. Or wait, was it three or four?"

"Who cares? Semantics. Laura, it's lovely to meet you. A friend of Sebastian's is a friend of mine." Lucas kissed the back of my hand, a tad forward if you ask me, but it didn't stop me from blushing.

"It's nice to meet you as well."

"Are you here with anyone?" Sebastian put his arm around my lower back, his hand rubbing my hip.

"Come on, when have you known me to bring a date to a party? Actually, I'm only in town for a few days, visiting my sister. She just had a baby. I bumped into Cooper yesterday at that dive bar over on Merrill Ave., and he invited me to tonight's shindig. I can't say no to a party."

"Cooper, huh? Is he here? I mean, have you seen him yet?"

"No, I thought he'd be standing somewhere by you. But I must say, it seems you've upgraded." Lucas winked at me with a lopsided smile. Creepy.

"Well, Lucas, we must carry on. We have matters to attend to. Company party and all. Let's catch up later, though. I expect I'll find you at the bar with three olives in a martini glass."

"You know me." Lucas shrugged with his palms facing the ceiling and walked away.

"He seems nice."

"He's a bit on the wild side, but he's a good guy. He helped me through a lot of messy situations. Oh, there's Matt. Come on."

This would be my first time meeting Matt. He stood at the bar, was shorter than I'd expected, had a square face, a rigid jawline, and a nasty scar on his left temple.

Sebastian shook his hand. "Little early for gin, isn't it?"

"Don't let the lime fool you. It's just water."

"Are we all set?"

"We're good."

Nobody was paying attention to me, so I peeked over my shoulders and looked around the room. Jake waved me over. I had little interest in talking to him but still felt bad about letting him down at dinner that night. I told Sebastian I'd be right back, pointed at Jake, who was only ten feet or so behind us, and, reluctantly, Sebastian said to go ahead and say hi but not to be gone long because I was needed in fifteen minutes, so we could go over the plan one last time.

"Hey, Laura." Jake hugged me. I halfheartedly put my hands on his back.

"How are you?"

"I'm great. But look at you. Wow. You look fantastic."

"Thank you." I smiled as I used to when waiting tables during my first year in college.

"I wanted to apologize for how I behaved at dinner. I don't know what I expected. I guess I let my imagination get the best of me. And then . . . hold on . . . oh, crap. Why did I volunteer to help coordinate this thing?"

"Everything okay?"

"It's Tommy, our liquor guy. They sent us the wrong order earlier. It was short about thirty cases. Both bars are almost out of champagne and Grey Goose. Apparently that's what passes for good vodka nowadays. Anyway, I've gotta run. Unless . . . you could give me a hand. It'll only take a minute, and then we can finish talking."

"I—I would but . . . I should really get back to Sebastian. I sort of ditched him before he even introduced me to his friend and, you know. . . ."

"I understand. I mean, it'll take me a little longer, what with Tommy's bum leg and all, and I'm sure someday I'll get a chance to finish my apology to you when I come back to visit my family on the holidays—"

"Wait, what? Are you moving?"

"Yeah, yesterday was my last day at Anderson Tech. Bianca even threw me a little going away party in the breakroom. I'm surprised she didn't tell you about it."

"I've been busy. We haven't talked for a few days. Gosh, I can't believe you're leaving. So this is goodbye then? Where're you moving to?"

"Oh, uh . . . Portland. Yeah, Portland, Maine. I've always loved the culture there. I've got a second-floor studio right by the harbor. Anyway, I better get going. Take care of yourself."

Jake turned to walk away, and impulse got the best of me. "Hey, wait up. I might as well give you a hand. Otherwise, my last memory of you will be of me refusing to help you, and the guilt will kill me for months."

"You sure? I mean, that would be helpful. It's only right through this side door over here, not far. A couple of trips and we'll be done."

"I'll follow you."

LAURA

I know it was stupid, and I should've returned to Sebastian, but it's not like I was going very far. The door was at the end of the hallway, just past the restrooms and elevators, right around the corner from Sebastian and Matt.

"Isn't this an emergency exit?"

"Yeah, but it's used for deliveries all the time. Don't worry, the alarm is turned off."

I stepped into the alleyway. A transit van with its sliding door opened waited just outside the doorway. "Hey, there's nothing in here. Maybe somebody already brought it—" A cloth smelling of chemicals covered my nose and mouth. I wanted to scream.

22

Sebastian

"What time you got?"

"Quarter of."

"We should get moving. I'll let Laura know we're taking our positions and reassure her we've got her covered from every angle. Meet me outside the elevators on the second floor. It might look weird if we go at the same time."

"Okay. See you in a minute."

But where was Laura? I turned around, and she and Jake were gone. I didn't see them anywhere. I walked around, weaving through pockets of people dressed in tuxedos and suits, dresses and gowns, jewelry, heavy makeup, champagne flutes, martinis glasses, and waiters with bad manners carrying trays. I saw Cooper sitting at the bar across the room. I couldn't ask him. Why was I surprised to see him? It was his company.

An elevator door closed. I opened the women's room door. "Laura. Laura, are you in here?"

"Get lost, creep."

Shit. Maybe she was already upstairs, waiting for me and Matt. No, that didn't make sense. Why would she do that? Fuck. I told her not to leave my side. Why did I let her go talk to that fucking weasel?

The elevator smelled like cigarette smoke. The doors slid open. Stepping onto the second floor gave me a sense of doom. "Matt, you in here?"

"Third stall, the handicap one. I'm dressed. Just pulling up the feed to the women's room door on my phone."

"Have you seen Laura?"

"No, did you check next door?"

"Not yet. I'm afraid to. I've checked everywhere else. I thought I'd ask you first."

"Well, we don't have a camera in the bathroom, for legal reasons, obviously, so you'll have to go in."

"I'll be back."

In the women's room, I checked the stalls. The third one wouldn't open, and though I couldn't see any heels and legs, I got down on my hands and knees and poked my head beneath the partition. Nothing, of course. I looked in a mirror, splashed cold water on my face, and watched it drip while attempting to process the situation.

Fuck.

"Matt, I think she's gone."

"You think they got to her already?"

"Let's go to the security room and check the footage."

"Should we tell the police first?"

"No, not till we know what's going on."

"What're we waiting for?"

"I'm just . . . I don't understand. How could I let this happen? All the planning, the safety measures, cops and undercover agents—and she gets picked off from right under our noses? Fuck, man."

Matt sat before the monitors and worked some magic, clicking and typing. He soon had the footage from the last hour inside the lobby, a total of eleven cameras. We watched Laura walk away from me and over to Jake. She followed him to the hallway near the bar we'd been sitting at. How the fuck did I miss it? For crying out loud, I was facing the hallway's entrance. "Pull that footage up. Shit. You've got to be kidding me. I knew there was something off about that guy."

"Looks like we found your mole. Hold up, I'll pull up the footage from the alley."

"Son of a bitch. Can you get the plate on the van?"

"Even if I could zoom in, the angle's shit. It would only give us a partial, and there must be thousands of those vans in this city alone."

"What a fuckin' mess. Let's go."

"Police?"

"Cooper's at the bar. Maybe he saw something."

"He's gonna kill you."

"Be that as it may, I have to find her, and if Cooper saw anything that might be helpful, I need to know."

In the elevator, a man held a woman's hand. Her dress was ruffled, clinging to her upper thigh on one side, showing some leg. She had a Post-It note stuck to her back.

Cooper was still at the bar, sitting sideways on the stool, his back to us.

I tapped him on the shoulder.

He spun around. "I'm just here to make sure nothing happens to my sister. So please, spare me your bullshit apology."

"Why would I need to apologize? That's ridic—you know what, never mind that. Did you see Laura leave with Jake?"

"Yeah, why? What do you care? You must have a dozen women you're fucking right now. What do you need with my sister?"

"Coop—I need you to be a sane, rational human being right now. Put the bullshit angst aside for a moment and work with me. Jake was a mole. I didn't know that thirty minutes ago. I knew there was a spy working here but didn't know who till now. Cooper—Laura has been taken. Do you understand? Because right now you don't look like a man who fully grasps the gravity of the situation. Now tell me, did you see anything unusual around the time Laura left with Jake?"

"You fucking asshole. I told you not to use her as bait. But you wouldn't listen. I should wring your neck right here in front of everybody. Did you even stop to consider what might happen to Laura if she was nabbed? Jesus fuck, she's probably halfway to Russia by now."

"Did you see anything unusual?"

"No, nothing. I thought she was running off to fuck Jake, which made me happy because it wasn't you. And because I saw her leave with him, I thought maybe you'd found another way to save her life. I mean, why else would you let her leave your side, you dumb fuck? Now what'd you plan to do?"

"Now we go to the police. Matt, find out where the UCs were when this happened. I want answers. I'll talk to the locals, report the incident, and see if they can pull up any footage of the van on traffic cams. Cooper, go home, see if you can login into her laptop. Maybe we can track her phone."

"The last I saw of the undercovers was when we were sitting at the bar. Sebastian, I think they're gone. I think—"

"Don't say it. We know nothing right now. Let's not make any costly assumptions. Coop, you with me?"

"Let's get one thing clear: I am not 'with you.' This is my sister, and I'll do whatever it takes to find her. I'll deal with you later."

"Good. Matt, call me in an hour with an update. Cooper, stop drinking."

23

Laura

Blink.

Blink-blink.

I'm not dead but nearly wishing it were so, coming to, drowsy in a torn black dress. Scathed knees. My ankles are tied to a chair's legs. I'm missing a shoe, damp dirt floor underfoot. I'm woozy. My head aches and drops back, swaying on a sore neck. To my right is the top of a staircase descending into darkness. Heavy breathing haunts the shadows. A scent reminiscent of burnt marshmallows nauseates me. I envision a child's arm holding a stick with a flaming white blob turning black and bubbling in a campfire and almost muster a sense of nostalgic joy until my head dips and the yellow light from a bare bulb with a pull string shoots needles into my eyes.

Above the glare is pink insulation drooping from the ceiling in curves like hills. Looking at it gives me an itch, which can't be scratched because rough rope holds my wrists together behind the chair. I am surrounded by stone walls with holes and crevices, some missing their faces. Pebbles and white dust from the walls crumbling have landed on the dirt and formed splash art. A piece of cardboard covers a rectangular window near the ceiling. Behind me, something drips steadily and competes with the dueling throbs of my head and heart.

Feet shuffle near the shadowed staircase. A lighter's flame scorches tinfoil and shows a flash of a face with a straw in its mouth. The flame collapses. Darkness hides the face. Seconds pass, and I hear a loud exhale. Evil steps into the light, wearing a familiar face.

"'Bout time. I've been waiting for you to wake up. How you feeling?"

"Go to hell, Jake."

"Don't bother struggling. I tied those knots myself. They're not coming undone."

"What do you want from me?"

He kneeled before me, placing a square piece of charred tinfoil on the dirt floor. On top of it, he set a pen's blue casing. One end showed a little white from where it was cut in half. He peered up at me. "I think you know exactly why you're here." He ran the back of his hand over my cheek. "Don't you." His fingers dragged through my cleavage. I shivered.

"Keep your hands off me, you creep." I spat on his face.

He grinned. "Ooh, aren't you a vicious little one." He sleeve-wiped his face. "I tell you what, if you can tell me where the thumb drive is, I'll let you go right now, no questions asked. But if you don't, well. . . ."

"You idiot. Why would Sebastian tell me where it is? Why? You've taken me for no reason. I can't help you. I don't have the information you want. Now let me go."

He stood, leaned over me, and grabbed my hair, tugging my head back. He quietly spoke through grinding teeth, his mouth beside my ear. "Either you're very stupid, or you're just pretending to be. Doesn't matter. I will get that drive. Sebastian won't have a choice now but to hand it over. In the meantime . . ." his tongue curled out and licked under my chin. "Maybe we can have a little fun."

"You're disgusting."

"You weren't saying that on our date. Remember our date, when you kissed me?"

"You kissed me. I was only being polite. Besides, that was back when I thought you were nice—not this lunatic who can only get a girl by kidnapping her."

"Do you know how hard it was for me to be Jake? What a bore. A pathetic loser. I'm glad that's over." He moved his hand beneath my dress, feeling up my leg, my thigh. "Mm, you are something else." He slipped a finger under my panties. Footsteps creaked the stairs.

"Is everything in order?"

Jake jumped up and stepped away from me. "Yes, boss. No issues with the package. Though she is a little feisty."

"Is that so." The man stepped into view, wearing a burgundy sports coat, a v-neck t-shirt tucked in, his belly fat bulging. Around his neck was a thin gold chain, a cross for a pendant. Black stubble, graying on the chin. He chewed on a toothpick, his hair slicked back. "Well, let me have a look at you. Very niiice. Junior, you weren't kidding. This one's a real beauty. Makes me wish we didn't need that thumb drive. Wouldn't mind keeping this one for myself." He hunched down and pushed my hair back, petting me. "What d'ya say, Laura. You wanna leave your boyfriend and be my pet?" His tongue flicked the toothpick, shifting it to his mouth's other corner. His breath smelled of cheap vodka, a strong cologne wafting from him.

"Junior." He stood, not taking his eyes off me. "Make the call. Tell Delarossi we have his woman and that if he wants her back, he knows what to do."

"On it, boss."

"Oh, and Junior . . . don't let me catch you smoking that shit on the job again. You need to be sharp. Sebastian is not to be underestimated."

24

Sebastian

Nothing, that was what we turned up, absolutely nothing. The undercover agents were on the take, I presumed. For all the smarts Matt had, he'd done a piss poor job of vetting the UCs. The city's traffic cams went offline two minutes before Laura's abduction and didn't return to working until exactly one hour later, unlikely a coincidence. And Cooper couldn't get into Laura's laptop, so that was a bust, too.

Six hours had passed. I was sick of sitting around but didn't know where to look. I paced the living room, trying to brainstorm. My anger disrupted my thoughts.

The phone rang, an unknown number.

"Yes."

"Mr. Delarossi. Do you know who this is?"

"Jake—I will burn down this entire fucking city and kill everybody that gets in my way. You can't stop me. Land or sea, there is nowhere I won't find you. So you might as well just tell me where she is now, and maybe I'll let you live."

"You forget who you're dealing with. You know my employer's reach exceeds yours by far. If you don't hand over the thumb drive, your precious Laura will be sold to some millionaire pervert overseas who'll fuck the pretty out of her, then sell her to a local pimp for a few grand and a free fuck at a whorehouse. You'll never find her. These girls don't get found. They get fucked until they're unfuckable, wind up giving blow jobs for smack in some shit city like Bangkok, then die of an overdose. This is Laura's future. If you want a better life for her, I suggest you play by the rules."

"Fine. We'll do it the hard way." I ended the call. Why not? He wouldn't give me Laura's location, so what was the point? Besides, I knew he'd call back in less than a minute. He hadn't given me his terms. And I needed a minute to think, of what, I didn't know. I had no plan and was without leads. Jake had the upper hand, and he knew it.

"Hey asshole. Who were you just talking to?"

"Jake."

"Does he have my sister?"

"I don't know. I hung up on him."

"You did what? Why the fuck would you do that? That's our first contact. Were up shit's creek, and you hang up?"

"Relax. He'll call—"

"You ready to give her back?"

"You and I both know that's not happening. You haven't a leg to stand on. Just hand over the drive and this all ends. Tomorrow. One p.m. Meet me at the abandon industrial complex. The last warehouse on the left. No cops. You come alone. Got it?"

"And if I don't?"

"We sell her to the highest bidder. And you know how that story ends."

Matt walked into the living room and whispered in my ear.

"It appears I have no other options. You win, Jake. I'll bring the thumb drive tomorrow."

"No cops."

"No cops."

"Don't fuck this up, Sebastian. They will kill you."

I ended the call.

"Matt, I thought you were doing recon."

"I was. I am. That's why I'm here. Listen, my guy said there's an auction in three days. If we can get somebody to pose as a buyer, my guy can get him on the guest list. We buy Laura back, and keep the drive. But it won't be cheap."

Cooper: "Money's no issue. But who'll be the buyer? They know our faces."

"Matt, will you do it?"

"On one condition: We bring the cops and take down the entire operation. No women get left behind. Once we have Laura and she's safely out of there, we let the cops do their thing. Deal?"

"Deal."

"Deal."

25

Laura

All night, drip—drip—drip, and it seemed to get louder as the night progressed. I'd dozed a few times yet hadn't slept. My back ached, and my wrists and ankles burned whenever I shifted my body because the ropes felt like serrated blades sawing into my flesh. The light bulb hanging from the ceiling before me hummed so quietly that it seemed to scream. Mice scurried about, squeaking. One would occasionally scuttle below the chair and between my feet. The dirt floor touching my shoeless foot reminded me of a fresh burial after a light rain because I imagined my funeral and knew it would be below a gray sky with mist spitting. I would die. I'd come to terms with that. Expect the worst, and you won't be let down. My mother taught me that.

Jake came down with a bowl of oatmeal and tried to spoon-feed me. I wouldn't open my mouth. Tight-lipped, I shook my head, squirming, fighting the tears from the razor-blade sensation the ropes gave me.

"You don't wanna eat. Fine with me. Go hungry. Buyers like women real skinny. Or maybe they've just grown accustomed to malnourished women and now prefer them. Know what I mean? C'mon, open up. This is your last chance."

I told him to bite me. He threw the bowl against the stonewall. Oatmeal splattered everywhere, food for the mice. He left, huffing up the stairs, and returned a while later with a bottled water. "Tilt your head back." My neck pinched a nerve and shot a shocking throb into the back of my head. Still, it was the best water I'd ever tasted. I drank it all except for what spilled down my cheeks and chin and dribbled onto my lap, wetting my dress. The water was warm but cold on my thighs.

Jake tossed the empty plastic bottle over his shoulder, said nothing, and walked away.

"Wait. I have to pee."

"So pee. I'm not stopping you."

A long time passed. I'd dozed once and woke to a mouse nibbling on one of my big toes. I still hadn't peed and had nearly reached my limit. I would burst any second.

Jake came down, bent low, and started untying my ankles. He hadn't shown much interest in me since the previous night. "Don't try anything, or I'll beat you senseless and have my way with you. Got it?"

"Are you letting me go?"

"We're going for a little ride. That's all. Maybe you go home. Maybe you don't. That's up to Sebastian."

"But I still have to pee."

As he walked around me, I saw he had a black-handled gun tucked into his pants. "There. You can stand now. If you want, you can squat in the corner over there, but I'm not leaving. I have to keep an eye on you."

"Can you at least turn around while I, you know, go?"

"No. I'm watching every drop."

I kicked off my one shoe to walk evenly and went by a corner near the stairway, partially hidden by a shadow. Jake followed, said hold on, ran to the top of the stairs, and returned with a flashlight. He crouched down a few feet from me, eye level. Pee touched my bare feet. Mice squealed nearby.

"Do you enjoy watching women pee?"

"Not usually. But in this case, yes. I've been dying to get a peek at you. I've been instructed not to touch you. So this will have to do."

I pulled up my panties, wobbled when getting up, lightheaded. He asked me to turn around and blindfolded me with something rough, a hint of gasoline. He tied my hands in front of me and held my elbow as we walked up the flexible steps.

A third man was in the car, his voice scratchy and low. Jake sat beside me, occasionally caressing my thigh, each time moving his fingers closer to my pussy but abruptly stopping as though he were about to get caught. We sat parked for what I imagined was an hour or so. The men talked and bickered outside of the car. When they got back in, they seemed angry and cussed.

Jake tied me back to the chair, tighter this time. "Sebastian fucked up. You'll be sold in two days. This is the best it gets for you. Enjoy it while it lasts."

He left the blindfold on me. I counted 3,983 drips and fell asleep. Dinner was cold lo mein. I passed. Jake persisted, shoving noodles into my face, sauce on my chin. Oatmeal was for breakfast again. I swallowed a bite and spat the next spoonful on Jake. I wish I could've seen where it'd landed. He called me a whore and stormed off. I slept in spurts, waking to mice at my feet and men screaming above the pink insulation.

Cold water on my leg woke me. Women speaking Spanish. They stopped talking when they realized I was awake. Each worked a sponge on either of my legs. I quivered at first but calmed when realizing they meant no harm. And the water felt nice, like any breeze on a hot day. I asked their names. No answer. I wept.

The sound of water splashing from the wringing of a sponge was soothing, that slow trickle, like a fountain in a park on a summer day. I asked for their help. "Please, let me go, untie me, allow me to escape." No answer. They washed up to my panty line, gently pulling my dress up a tad. Then they wiped down my arms and under them. "Have some compassion. You both seem like nice people. Don't let them do this to me. Please. I'm begging you." I wept.

They pulled my dress's straps off my shoulders, shimmied the dress down near my waist, and unclasped my bra. Under, over, and around my breasts, they speechlessly dabbed the sponge. Then my back, my forehead, cheeks, and neck. Once they righted my dress, one said something. The other faintly said si, followed by the sound of sponges plopping into the bucket of water. I wept.

One of them delicately brushed my hair. The other applied makeup to my face, a swipe of lipstick. Steady, she said. She spoke English. Had they understood every word I'd said and chosen to ignore me? A knot in my hair, she tugged at it. "Hey, I'm desperate. I'll do anything. Please. All you have to do is untie me. You can say I was here when you left and pretend you know nothing. I'll pay you. Whatever you want. You can buy new lives and get away from these assholes. Ple-ee-ease." They left. I wept

I cried until I couldn't cry anymore, until my tear ducts dried and hope was forgotten. And I waited. What came next was obvious but not. I knew nothing of what lay ahead for me, yet I knew my existence would be forever altered, my body an object, my pussy worn whithered, unworthy again of a sane man, of Sebastian. Even if I were found a month or a year later and my life had been saved and returned to some semblance of normal, what life would I have? This was the death of Laura. I wept.

Jake put me in a car. He said I looked pretty and wished he had a chance to fuck me. Then he smacked my ass as I stepped up into the vehicle.

It was the same car. I could tell by the scented mixture of a pine-tree air freshener and stale cigarette smoke. And the leather seat I sat on had the same crack between my legs. Nobody said anything the entire ride. I pretended to look out the window and imagined purple lilacs lilting under a blue sky, greenery, and songbirds hidden in trees singing just for me. And quietly, I wept.

26

Laura

Once I was inside, wherever I was, Jake removed my blindfold, untied my wrists, and told me to undress. He handed me tattered lingerie, all balled up, smelling of sex and perfume. Sitting on a threadbare loveseat, he watched me change, staring intensely.

The room was small, had paint peeling, a hideous snot-green color, and many fist-sized holes in the walls. Empty liquor bottles, crushed beer cans, and crumpled cigarette boxes were scattered about the floor. The room smelled of piss.

Jake stood, removed a flask from his back pocket, and took a swig. "You want some? Calm the nerves."

I couldn't think of a reason not to. "Sure. Why not?"

As I tilted my head back, shaking out the flask's last drop, he grabbed my ass, aggressively rubbing one cheek. "How about we have a quickie before you leave? Something for you to remember me by."

"How about you go to hell." I tossed the flask onto the couch behind him and yanked his hand off my ass. Angered, he grabbed both ass cheeks and pulled me to him, as Sebastian had done many times. Jake kissed me. My lips played dead, my mouth sealed. His hand in my panties, he pulled it out, smelled his fingers, and sucked on two. "Mmm. Even without a shower for a few days, you taste good." He crouched, stroking my legs. "You don't have to do anything. I'm used to dead lays. But I think I have just enough time to—" The door opened. Jake jumped up.

"Junior. She's next. Let's go."

"Yes, boss."

The door closed.

"Too bad. I was just about to make you scream."

He walked me out by the arm, down a hallway with torn posters of old theatre shows. All that remained of some was a corner taped to the wall of the same snot-green paint.

Backstage, Jake padlocked a steel shackle around my right ankle. On the other side of the curtain, applause happened. A woman sobbed while walking toward me, coming off the stage. The chain she was shackled to ended at my feet, where a large ring bolt had been screwed into the floor. The woman wore black lingerie. She looked sixteen and dropped her chin when walking by me, wiping her eyes. On her ribcage was the number 12 written in black marker.

"Oh, I almost forgot. Lift your arm." Jake wrote a thirteen above my hip. A man with a cigarette behind one ear and a tight shirt showing off his bulging biceps unchained the woman and handed the chain's end to Jake. The men exchanged a nod. Jake attached the chain to the shackle around my right ankle and slapped my ass. "I wouldn't be surprised if you go for over a hundred grand. Go on, now. You're up."

Skittishly I walked toward center stage. A man wearing a red bowtie was on the stage's left, near the edge. He had gray hair, was well-groomed, old enough to be my grandfather, and stood at a podium with an electronic tablet. "Come along now, darling. Don't be scared. Nobody's going to hurt you." A microphone must've been clipped to his lapel. He waved me over. "Right there, sweetheart. Center stage, where everybody can see how beautiful you are. Up a little. Forward. That's it. Now give us a slow spin. That a girl."

Bright lights. Though squinting, I could still see the crowd. The buyers sat in the first four rows and wore Guy Fawkes masks. In their laps, they held numbered signs attached to sticks that looked like paint stirrers. The mezzanine remained empty. On its front wall, a banner hung with one corner folded over. The letters I could see read: **Endgam**.

"Buyers, are we ready? . . . I'll start the bidding at fifty thousand, anyone for fifty thousand? I see fifty thousand and fifty, sixty, sixty thousand and fifty, one hundred thousand, whoa, will anyone top one hundred thousand. . . . Going once. . . ."

Picture me on a stage, lights blaring, wearing red lingerie with the lace stretched and torn and my precious pussy nearly fully on display for a bunch of creeps wearing Guy Fawkes masks and my tears unstoppable. I didn't know what to do with my hands. What was I supposed to do with my hands? My inclination was to cover myself up, my palms on my breasts, legs crossed. Instead, I kept my hands by my side, digging my nails into my thighs, hoping a natural disaster would strike and topple the building and kill me.

"Going twice. . . . One hundred thousand and five hundred! Anyone for two hundred thousand? No? I see you thinking. Going once. . . . Anybody? . . . Going twice. . . ."

My legs shook numbly. I was nauseated and cold. Some of the men in the front row were rubbing themselves. One guy had his hand in his pants. Each wore the same black suit and bowtie and were indistinguishable from one another. To say I was afraid is an understatement. Piss dribbled down my legs.

"And we have two hundred thousand! Look at that. Keep it coming. She's a real beauty. Will anyone outbid two hundred thousand? . . . Anybody. . . . Going once. . . . Going twice. . . . Sold! to number 67 over in the back left corner for two hundred thousand dollars. You may claim your lady after the bidding's done. Next."

Moving off the stage, I moped, scraping my shoes against the worn wood, wobbling a bit because I was weak in the knees and unused to heels made for streetwalkers. Jake waved me along, trying to rush me. The chain connected to my ankle clanked as it folded and met. The men clapped, celebrating God knows what? God who? What a question to ponder at a time like this. Never mind that. Let's get on with it. The death of Laura Anderson.

Fuck weeping. This is it. I submit. I accept my fate and will not shed another tear for these men because I know they feed off weakness and fragility. I am strong but not. I know my place. I will play my role and lie down wherever I'm told. I will smile and survive but why? Because I will buy my time until I gather the strength and resources to end my life. That's right. I will kill myself.

Suicide was my only thought when Jake caressed my leg while unshackling my ankle. I had a plan. Knowing my demise was in my hands made me feel powerful. So when Jake brought me back to the room and watched me undress, I smiled and teased him with a lip bite, taunting him. Why? Because fuck him. And since I was now somebody's property, he couldn't have me. Sure, he could look, sneak a touch or a squeeze, but he couldn't have me. Weirdly, this comforted me.

"Now what? Are you going to whip out that little dick of yours and fuck me? Or are you a watcher? Yeah, I bet you like to watch." I ruffled his hair and rubbed his earlobe. "You wanna watch me undress again so you can beat off? Huh? Tell me Jake, what do you want me to do."

"Oh, Laura—Laura, Laura, Laura . . . as much as I would like to fuck you, you now belong to somebody. You should be worried, frightened even. You were. What happened? Did that whisky give you a little false courage, or is this just an act? Do you really think you can use your looks and sex to manipulate me or one of those guys into getting whatever you want? Well, I hate to break it to you, but that's not happening. Not in this world. In this world, you are the manipulated. Try all you want. It won't matter. These men buy, sell, and trade women daily. They don't give a shit about you. No feelings. No attachment. You are nothing but merchandise, a piece of ass. And like all products, you will wear old, and men will grow bored of you. By this time next year, you'll have been sold off a handful of times and be begging for the needle, just another hit to get right, and you'll take as many dicks as you have to to get it. I almost feel bad for you. Almost. If I were you, I'd smarten up.

Know your place. Speak when spoken to. Do as you're told. Keep him happy and when not fucking, make like a ghost."

"I hate you. You did this to me. You, you fucking prick. I hope you die choking on your own blood, and I hope Sebastian is the one standing over you, smirking, saying, I told you so. Fuck you." I spat on him. Why not? It felt great the first time, and I was on fire. I wasn't afraid of Jake. Jake was still a weasel. Except this Jake was a perverted weasel who played a gopher to men stronger than him. He was nothing. Nobody.

He wiped my saliva from his eye without a grin.

The door opened.

"Hey, boss. Just keeping an eye on her."

"Junior, you're no longer needed here."

"Right. I'll wait outside."

"No. Go home. Your services are no longer needed. Find a new job. Now beat it."

"Yes, bo—yes, sir."

"Laura, I have somebody here who would like to meet you."

Guy Fawkes entered the room. Jake's boss closed the door. Fawkes was wordless. He grabbed my hand as if I were in danger and said, "We need to leave. Now."

We walked through the hallway, going away from the stage. Fawkes seemed rushed and anxious. We took a left at the end of the hall, then a right, then we were in an alleyway beside a turned-over metal trash can blackened and dented. He held my hand, jogging. I kicked off my heels to keep pace with Fawkes and what seemed like an escape. At the end of the alley and to the left was a black SUV, shiny under a full moon. He opened the rear door and told me to get in. I did. He ran to the passenger side, hopped into the vehicle, and sat beside me. I couldn't see the driver's face because I was sitting behind him. But I noticed he wasn't wearing a mask.

"Drive," said Fawkes. The SUV pulled forward and came out of the alleyway onto the main street of a small town abandoned for the night or forever. The only working streetlamp flickered. Fawkes began to remove his mask.

LAURA

Police cars zipped out from side streets and unseen places farther up the road, silent sirens and lights spinning blue flashes. The police cars sped past us, going toward the theatre. My head whipped around, mouth gaped. A black SUV moved fast behind us, either chasing or catching up to us. "Laura." The police cars rushed by the black SUV. "Laura." That my name was being said by a strange man didn't seem unordinary for some reason. Our SUV picked up speed, and the one behind us did the same, closing the gap between us. So many thoughts tangled my mind. "Laura!"

"What?" I shouted.

"Laura, look at me."

"Matt? . . . Matt! Holy shit! But what are you doing here? I thought . . . what the hell is going on?"

"Shh, take a breath. Relax. You're safe now. . . . Breathe, Laura, breathe."

"Wait, where's Sebastian?"

"He's fine. That's him behind—"

Over Matt's shoulder, a storefront window reflected a cloud of hellish orange expanding upward and outward from the SUV trailing us. Its front end leaped several feet off the pavement. It happened quickly but slowly, our seat vibrating. With the deafening boom accompanying the explosion came the sound of metal clattering within our vehicle. Shrinking my neck and raising my shoulders, I covered my ears. Our vehicle slowed to a stop. Matt told the driver to keep going and that there was nothing we could do. Not until later, while warming my hands around a styrofoam cup and staring at the wrong side of a one-way mirror, did I realize what Matt had meant when he said there was nothing we could do: You can't save the dead.

27

Laura

For three days, I prayed to a god I should've believed in. The fourth day was as sunny as the previous three, too bright for me to step outside, which I only knew because I could see sunlight cutting between the wall and the curtain's outer edges, laying a stripe over my dresser.

A knock on the door. "Can I come in?"

"Go away."

"I have breakfast. Blueberry waffles, your favorite."

"I'm not hungry."

"You have to eat at some point. You can't live like this forever."

"Good."

"You don't mean that. . . . I'm coming in, whether you like it or not. I'll give you a minute to get decent."

The doorbell rang.

"You lucked out, for now. I'll be back, and then we'll sit down and have a nice breakfast together. Okay? . . . I'll take your silence as a yes."

Once I could no longer hear Cooper's boots thumping on the hardwood floor of the hallway, I tossed off the comforter and ran to the window, pulling a curtain a smidgen away from the window's frame to see who waited at the front door. Two uniformed officers stood chatting casually a few feet from the unpruned butterfly bush near the steps. A moment later, Cooper let them inside.

I cracked my bedroom door, hoping to overhear their conversation, and only heard my heart's accelerating pitter-patter. I tip-toed down the hall and crouched at the top of the stairway, my nightgown scraping my feet. They were in the kitchen, to the left of the stairway's bottom landing.

"With all due respect, officers, can we skip the pleasantries and get to the point? Were the remains his or not?"

"According to the dental records, yes. It's Sebastian. I—I'm sorry for your loss."

I covered my mouth and couldn't decide whether to in- or exhale, choking on a breath, holding it, and gradually losing temperance. I clung to the banister and dropped onto my ass's side, my legs bent and scissored. I released the held breath and tried to fill my lungs while exhaling.

Cooper told the officers to wait a minute and that he'd be right back.

"Laura, you should go back in your room. I'll be up in a minute." Cooper walked away, his head downturned.

I couldn't move.

"What about the thumb drive, any luck finding that?"

"It was in his left boot. The heel had a false bottom. The detectives who discovered it, said it was melted onto the rubber, destroyed. We couldn't retrieve the files."

"Shit. But you didn't need them, did you? I mean—you were able to nail the traffickers during the sting at the auction, right?"

"I'm sorry. We can't comment on an ongoing investigation."

"Ongoing? Are you fucking kidding me? So those assholes are still out there? Bravo . . . (light clapping) . . . That's just fucking fantastic. You were handed this thing on a silver platter, and still, you can't lock them up. Unbelievable. So my friend died for what, so these guys can rape and pillage the world while you scoff doughnuts to kill time till your pensions arrive?"

"We understand your frustration. And I promise you, we're doing everything we can to take these guys down. But investigations of this caliber are complex and tend to take a while. It's not the best system, but it's all we've got."

"Great. Keep up the good work, fellas. . . . Anything else? . . . No? You know where the door is."

I ran back to my room, slammed the door, and buried my face in a pillow. Cooper came in and sat beside me on the bed, rubbing my back, a gesture he'd never before done.

"Listen, Laura, Sebastian was a good man. I know I said some things out of anger, but I didn't mean them. He was like a brother to me. I loved him, and he will be missed. Now, I don't know the depth of the relationship between you two, but it's clear you cared for him a lot. This will be a difficult time for both of us. The best we can do is remember him. And you know he wouldn't want us to have our lives stand still. Let's grieve, yes, but let's not allow our grieving to control our daily lives. Does that make sense? . . . Laura?"

"I can't. . . . I can't. I can't. I can't. Just go away. Please. I'm begging you. Leave me be."

An hour passed. A day. A week. Time was irrelevant. I finally showered. The water felt good, and then it didn't because feeling good while Sebastian was dead seemed like a crime. I stepped out of the shower, refreshed and ashamed. Walking into my bedroom, I was startled. Bianca sat at the foot of my bed. She'd drawn the curtains. The sunlight was unbearable.

"What are you doing here?"

"I wanted to check up on you, see how you were doing. You haven't returned any of my calls or texts. I'm worried about you. That's all."

"I'm fine."

"You wanna go grab some lunch? We could snag some burritos from that food truck you love and walk the promenade."

"I'm not hungry."

"We could walk around the neighborhood and talk. We don't have to go far, just get some fresh air. It'll do you good. I promise."

"Pass."

"C'mon. You can't just stay in your room for the rest of your life. How about a movie? Yeah, we don't even have to leave the house. I'll pop some popcorn and we can be lazy on the couch and watch your favorite movie. What is your favorite movie? Gosh, there's so much I don't know about you."

"*Breakfast at Tiffany's.*"

"Really. Why? Nothing even happens in that movie."

"That's what I thought, too, when Cooper introduced me to it. I was like twelve. Then I watched it a bunch of times because my parents didn't want me to and fell in love with it."

"Well, I haven't seen it in ages, so maybe I'll like it this time around. What d'ya say?"

"Fine. But only if there's wine. I haven't had a drink all week."

"I'll go get everything ready while you finish toweling your hair and whatnot. White or red?"

"Both."

"That a girl."

"Don't say that."

"Say what?"

"'That a girl.'"

"Why not?"

"Because I'm asking you not to. That's why. Now go. I need to be alone for a minute. I'll be down in a bit."

"Uh, okay. You sure you're alright?"

"Go."

Brushing my hair before the full-length mirror, I thought of my red dress, how that night, while putting on my earrings in this same spot, my mirrored smile had lured Sebastian closer to me. He had such a big grin. I'd never seen him look so happy. Just thinking of it all, I could feel his hands caressing my ass. The goosebumps were real.

I set the brush on the dresser beside the full-length mirror while glaring at my reflection. The longer I stared at the mirror, the more I seemed to remember, the more real he felt. I tried to imagine him here now, his fingers on my clit, rubbing it in circles the way he always had. That hand. Fuck. The pool, where it all began, and I became a slave to that hand. My pussy was as alive now as it was then, bursting with wet throbs. His hand was my hand, and my hand was in my pants, massaging my clit with my bottom lip bit.

I teased myself with a couple of fingertips, then slipped three fingers in my pussy because that's how many Sebastian would've used. Thinking of his hard cock, I watched my reflection play with herself. I grabbed one of my breasts and squeezed it too hard. I needed a little pain, his hand on my throat. My hand on my throat, slowing my breathing with a pinch. I pushed my thumb deeper into my larynx. A world without Sebastian is a world I don't want to fuck in. My fingers in my pussy moved faster. I envisioned Sebastian on top of me, slamming his cock into my pussy, choking me. His thrusts, fast and hard, made me want to scream, even in this wide-awake dream. I felt the vibration of a moan wither against my thumb while my fingers down south worked with the speed of Sebastian's cock pounding into my pussy. I put more pressure on my throat and fiddled with my pulsing clit, massaging it, pushing my palm downward against my clit and lips, then dragging my middle finger upward, sneaking a fingertip in my pussy on the way by. That hand on my throat. My face pale. The throb of my clit between thumb and forefinger, a twist, and I quit.

I sat in the desk chair to catch my breath, my forearms on the armrests. Panting and eerily serious, I glared at the mirror and said, "Good girl." My jeans were wet, bordering on soaked. Once my breathing slowed, I saw the glistening juices on my hand. I licked my palm and sucked as Sebastian would've done on my fingers and moaned as if trying to summon him from the dead, a deep and passionate moan that skipped my heart a beat. Then the doorbell rang.

Bianca came running up the stairs and burst into my bedroom. "Laura! Laura! You will never fucking believe who's here. I mean—never. Holy fuck."

28

Laura

I told Bianca I'd be down in a minute. She pleaded, holding my hands and bouncing on her heels. I couldn't comprehend her excitement because it meant nothing to me, and neither did the mystery visitor. I already had one uninvited guest. Why would I want another?

I said I had to change my clothes. She didn't understand. I explained I had an accident—that was all—just an accident, and I showed her the front of my pants, warning her not to ask questions. It was embarrassing, except I didn't feel embarrassed. She said she'd wait downstairs and dashed away.

I undressed in the bathroom, wet a washcloth, washed myself, and dressed in dry clothes. I looked in the mirror for a creepy minute and laughed a weird laugh, a cackle with a suspicious grin. Had I gone mad? Good. I'd take mad over sad any day of the week. I opened the medicine cabinet as though looking in the fridge for anything to eat. A can of Barbasol in hand, I squirted a dab in my palm and smelled it. I looked heavenward and closed my eyes, inhaling. I smiled while holding my breath, waiting for his ghost to say something new, a sign of some sort, telling me what to do next. How to move on. Where I belong. Then a knock on the door twitched my skin. "I'll be out in a minute."

Another three taps on the door happened.

"I said—I'll be out in a minute. Go away."

Another three taps. I growled, flung the door open, and stood motionless, staring. I was happy for a second, then confused, then I slapped him. Shaving cream splattered back, a dollop landing on my chin. "Asshole."

Sebastian grinned.

I slapped him again. Splat went the shaving cream. "Do you have any idea what you've put me through? Do you? Stop smiling. I have been an emotional fucking wreck, grieving your death, and all the while you've been al—" He kissed me. His embrace was tight and warm. Despite the anger and unresolved grieving, I was ecstatic and wet.

After a brief tongue battle, I pulled back. "You have some serious explaining to do. I'm mad at y—" He kissed me.

After a long tongue battle, his stubble grating my face, I pulled back. "Will you please tell me what hell is—" He kissed me.

After tiring our tongues and letting our hands wander, his stubble burning my face, I pulled back. "Now—tell me why, why did I have to go through all—" He kissed me.

After tiring our tongues and letting our hands wander into moans, I couldn't feel his stubble grating my face anymore. Every muscle in my body gave out. Limp, I nearly fell.

"I missed you."

"You're a jerk."

"Come. Everybody's waiting downstairs. I'll explain everything." He grabbed my hand and led me to the stairs.

"No. You better tell me something right this minute that will make sense of all this. Make something up if you have to, but I won't walk any farther without an explanation."

"I had to, okay. It was the only way to catch the traffickers. Now please, come downstairs, and I'll tell you every detail along with the beginning of what I imagine will be a very long apology."

"Did you catch them? You better have fucking caught them after all this."

"Yes, we caught them. Now, would you. . . . " He pulled me down the stairway and released my hand before turning the corner into the kitchen, where Matt, Cooper, and Bianca sat at the island around a pot of coffee.

Cooper: "Enough with the suspense. We overheard the why, now tell us the how."

"Okay, where do I start? . . . That night, the night of the auction, I sat in a dumpster in the alleyway, about a hundred feet away from the trafficker's fleet of SUVs. I watched their comings and goings through the cardboard slot. Anyway, a few days before the auction, I'd rented two black SUVs that matched their fleet, one for Matt, one for me. I parked mine in the alley with theirs, hoping nobody would notice the extra vehicle. I thought having the SUV close by would allow me a quick escape.

Matt: "So what happened?"

"I'm getting there. During the auction, Jake came out, slid beneath the front end of my SUV, and planted explosives. He then went to the SUV in front of mine, grabbed a cigarette from a box on the dash, smoked it, and went back inside. I scrambled over, removed the C-4 and planted it on Jake's SUV. I assumed the timer on it was set, but without electricity I couldn't know for how many minutes. So I had no idea how long it would take once the car started for it to blow."

Me: "Wait, so that was Jake who died in that car?"

"Yup. Stupid son of a bitch. I'd planned to follow you guys when you left, which was why Matt assumed it was me, but I didn't get out of the dumpster in time. Jake must've caught wind that something was up with Laura's buyer, maybe because they left in such a hurry. Who knows? We can't interrogate him to find out. What's interesting, though, is we learned the organization had fired Jake after Laura was bought, so we wondered if maybe he thought catching Laura might get him his job back."

Me: "Can we skip to that part where you have to pretend to be dead?"

"Yeah, I didn't want to do that. But it was the only way. When the cops arrived at the theatre, the only remaining people in the building were a few buyers who'd lost out in the auction. Somebody tipped off the traffickers. We think they had men on the roof as lookouts. Anyway, after talking with agents on the scene, we came to the conclusion that me being dead, and the thumb drive gone, would make the traffickers think they had nothing to worry about: no drive, no case. We just had to make them believe I was dead for a while and track their movements. We finally nailed them at an auction in Oakland, their last one before heading back overseas. By we, I mean the authorities. I've been in a safe house this entire time, no internet connection, no cable, and no phones—total darkness."

Me: "Were the women saved?"

"Yes, they saved fifteen women at the auction and were led by a snitch to thirty two women who were locked up in a shipping container headed for Germany the next morning."

Matt: "For the record, I knew nothing about this. I thought what you guys thought, that he was dead and gone. This is some serious movie-type shit. I'm both impressed and pissed off. And I missed out on all the fun."

"I wouldn't call sitting in a cabin out in nowhere drinking excessive amounts of coffee while your closest friends grieved your death fun. It was difficult, to say the least. From the bottom of my heart, I'm sorry for what I put you all through. I really am."

Cooper: "I think you owe my sister the biggest apology. Let's be clear, I'm in no way condoning whatever you two have, nor do I think it should continue, but what she went through over the last week was unbearable to watch. I can only imagine how she felt and how she feels now. I was worried she might try to harm herself."

"Cooper, at some point, you and I should sit down with a bottle of scotch and talk. I'll leave it at that for now. And I know I owe Laura an immense apology, several probably."

Me: "You're damn right you do."

"Laura, I helped a lot of women by doing what I did, gave them freedom and hope. It kills me that I had to fake my death to do it and put you, all of you, through such emotional hell, but it was for a good cause."

Cooper: "We're glad to have you back."

"You guys didn't have my funeral, did you?"

Cooper: "We were holding off, trying to find a way to contact your folks. We didn't want to do it without them, you know? I'd planned to wait another week and then set a date, whether I'd got in touch with them or not. I'd already purchased a casket and burial plot, though. I'll send you the bill."

"Send it to the F.B.I."

Me: "It can still be arranged you know?"

"What's that?"

"Your funeral."

"Could I have the room, please, so I can speak to Laura for a moment alone?"

Cooper whispered loudly in Sebastain's ear. "The best thing you could do for her right now would be to break it off. You know it, and I know it. She'll understand in due time." He patted Sebastian's shoulder. "Bianca, I'm pretty sure you're not Laura. Come on. Let's give them time to talk."

Bianca: "But I haven't had lunch. I'm starving."

Cooper: "Well, then let's go get something to eat. My treat. I'll even let you choose the restaurant."

Bianca: "Really? Can we take your Tesla? I've never been in one."

Cooper: "Sure. You can even drive if you want."

Bianca: "Lunch with the boss, and I get to drive his car . . . this is too good."

Me: Oh, God, will you two please leave. You're making me nauseous."

And then there were two.

The front door shut with a thud. Across the kitchen's island, we gazed at each other, staring intently. I didn't know what to expect. He swallowed and appeared to have something caught in his throat. These weren't fuck me eyes. I'd never seen this look on him. I was about to say something stupid when he spoke.

"I love you," he said.

And that was all the apology I needed.

Epilogue

"What are you doing?"

"Just sending out a few emails, letting some clients know I'll be on vacation for another week."

"Another week? But I thought you had to get back tomorrow?"

"Ehh . . . work can wait. Besides, look at this view. Hearing those waves at night has given me some of the best sleep I've ever had. We gotta come here more often."

"Like every weekend."

"I was thinking maybe a few times a year."

"With me?"

"Just you."

EPILOGUE

"You wanna go for a swim?"

"I've got a few more emails to send. Why don't you head down to the shore and get your feet wet, and I'll meet you there in a litle bit."

"Okay." She leaned over and gave me a kiss. Walking away, she stopped halfway down the deck's steps. "Hey, did you notice these lilacs here?"

"I did. Funny, isn't it?"

She had one leg on a higher step than the other, bent and gleaming. Her red bikini revealed an ass cheek without tan lines. "These ones here, the magenta, symbolize passionate, unbridled love."

I was unsure how to respond. I didn't think she wanted me to say anything, either. She was in her own world. Cupping a lilac, she caressed its petals with a thumb, lightly grazing over them, dazed.

She looked over at me, her smile faint but packed with bliss and serenity, her eyes full of marvel. "I did a paper on them in middle school. They're my favorite flower. Some say lilacs symbolize new beginnings and renewal. Or maybe that's the white ones. Does it matter?"

"What do you think?"

"I think the water's calling me. Don't be long." Walking down the steps, her ass bounced a bit, her ponytail waving.

I closed my laptop and traded it for my phone. I scrolled through my contacts, found the name I wanted, and stared at it, thinking of all the things I should say and everything I wouldn't. I tapped the call button and counted the rings. After the sixth, she answered. I immediately felt like a little boy.

"Mom. It's me. Sebastian."

This call was a long time coming, and the vulnerability and courage required to contact her affected me as much as hearing the relief and love in her voice. The emotions we shared were overwhelming, joyous, yet sorrowful. We kept our conversation basic; how are you; good, everything is well; it's so glad to hear your voice; yours too; we've been so worried; me too; does this mean it's safe, that we're safe, your father and I?; yes, yes it does. And in a brief sweep of words, I told her the threat was gone, and she and my dad no longer had to hide. They could come home if they wanted to. And they would. Dad said so himself. I talked to him, too. He misses me. He loves me. He's mad at me. He's dying. See you soon, son, if I make it. Then mom said farewell; hugs and kisses, talk soon. Love you. Bye. And I nearly cried.

I silenced my phone and set it beside my laptop on the end table. I went to the deck's railing, leaned on it, resting my weight on my forearms, and watched Laura come out of the ocean like an apparition. She was close enough to see me wave but too far away for us to swap words. But none were needed.

On our first night here, we'd shared our feelings, our hopes and dreams, the good and the bad, everything we had, and held nothing back. We were on the same page. We'd both been hurt, just like you, and we made that infamous promise not to break one another's heart and called it a start.

She claimed we harnessed a psychic connection, an invisible link that had brought us together, and nothing would tear it apart. I believed her. How could I not? And the more time I spent with her, fucking and talking and talking about fucking, the more powerful her presence became, the more it enthralled me, every touch, any look, each word, and I'd crumble internally.

EPILOGUE

She walked onto the deck, salty beads of water rolling down the curve of her hips and shoulders, glistening like a new car in the rain. "I thought you were coming down."

"I was. I'd planned to. You came back too soon. I was just taking it all in."

"You were watching me." She strutted over, one foot in front of the other, and put a hand on my back.

"I like watching you."

"I like it when you watch me. What's up? You look . . . deep in thought."

"I just got off the phone."

"And. . . ."

"I called my parents."

She rubbed my back. "Baby, that's awesome. I'm sure that took a lot of courage. Were they happy to hear from you?"

"Yes, though they were a little pissed I'd left them out there in hiding and hadn't kept in touch to let them know what was going on. I get it. I expected it. But it doesn't make it easier to bear."

"I'm proud of you. You've come a long way in the short time I've been, uh, working for you. Speaking of which, do I still work for you?"

"Let's just enjoy our time here together and worry about the real world when we return to it."

"I can get behind that—if you can get behind me...."

I pushed myself off the railing. "You don't have to tell me twice."

"Ooh, right here?"

"Right here." I pulled one end of her bikini's string on her back. She shrugged off her top, moving in front of me. I crouched, pushed my hands up her thighs and hips, touched a tit, and pulled off her bikini's bottom piece when gliding my hands back down. Then I bit her ass and licked the perfectly indented bite mark my front teeth left behind. She leaned on the railing as I had, forearms down, and wiggled her ass with a shimmy of the hips. Looking over her back, a hunger in her eyes, her tongue stretched out and whisked her lips, nearly touching her nose with its tip.

I rose, unbuckled my pants, and smacked her ass. Hard. She sucked in a breath and pushed out an *ooh*. I dropped my pants, stripped off my briefs, then teased her clit with the head of my hard dick. She shook off a quiver and looked back, her spine dipping into an elegant curve, the day's last sunlight kissing where her wings should be. And she grinned. My cock in her pussy, hands gripping her hips, I pulled her ass against me and tried to wiggle my way in deeper, pushing and pushing, my cock throbbing. She moaned into a lilac bush, magenta, and nudged me with her ass. Go time.

I pulled back. She bit her lip, looking at me instead of the twinkle of twilight giving birth to night and dropping shimmers across the ocean's face. Then her face whipped toward the stars because I slammed my cock into her pussy so hard her arms almost slipped off the rail. I fucked her harder than I'd ever fucked and then fucked harder. She screamed and squealed and squeaked, and when I rubbed her clit, she moaned in singsong. And just as I was about to come, she looked back at me mid-scream, stopped, and said, "This isn't love."

EPILOGUE

"Ugh. 'Bout time. You can ask questions later. Right now you need to untie me. We're going to miss our flight if we don't hurry."

"Untie . . . Shit. You've been like this all night?"

"Yeah. Don't worry, I asked you to tie me up. I just didn't predict you'd fall onto the floor, then say it was nice down there, and pass out."

"Hey, is my hungover brain making shit up, or did I see Bianca and Cooper getting cozy by the fire last night?"

"Damn, it feels good to use my limbs again. You're not imagining things. Now get dressed."

"Who's honking?"

"That's the limo. Are you alright? Hand me that dress on the lamp. The only one on a lamp. Yeah. But seriously, you seem . . . a little off."

"Strange dream."

"I'm glad we packed last night. Phew. I'll get the suitcases and meet you down there."

"Okay . . . Wait, no. I'll bring the suitcases down. You go say bye to your brother. I can't face him right now."

"He'll come around."

"I doubt it."

"Give it time. Okay. Meet you down there."

I was ready but felt I was missing something. I took a look around the room, a mess, for sure. I went to the closet, pulled my toy box down from the top shelf, and grabbed what Laura called "the pink thing." I slipped it into the inside pocket of my sports jacket, turned off the lamp, and lugged the suitcases downstairs.

"All set?"

"All set. Love you, Coop, bye—Bianca, I'll call you when we land. See ya."

As soon as Laura turned her back, Cooper gave me an unhappy look. "Right," I said. "See you guys in a week."

I jogged through the living room to catch up with Laura. "Hold up. Let me get the door."

"Your hands are full."

"Now they're not."

"Cute."

"Hey, don't let me forget, once we get settled in down there, I need to make a call."

"Sure. Should I be worried?"

"No. I'll tell you on the flight. Wait, just give me a second to hand these off to the driver, and I'll get your door."

EPILOGUE

"What's gotten into you?"

"Huh? Nothing."

I told the limo driver to raise the partition.

"Look what I brought?"

"Oh my."

I turned it on. "Drop your pants."

"Now!"

"Now."

I teased her for a second, my fingertips rubbing her lips. She was already slippery and moaning. I set the pink thing's circular part over her clit. "Hold that" I got on my knees before her. "Open your legs."

"Holy shit. Are you seriously about to do what I think?"

"I'll do whatever I want to you. Now, don't remove it unless I tell you to. Understand?" The limo took a hard right and jostled us a tad. "Open them wider."

"Like this?"

"Good girl."

Made in United States
North Haven, CT
27 December 2023

46693530R00093